THE
MARRIAGE

THE

MARRIAGE

by **Witold Gombrowicz**

Translated from the Polish by
Louis Iribarne

Northwestern University Press
Evanston, Illinois

Originally published as *Ślub* in the Polish-language review *Kultura* (Paris, 1953). This translation is based on the revised edition published in 1957 (Czytelnik, Warsaw), under the title *Transatlantyk—Ślub* (i.e. Gombrowicz's novel *Transatlantyk* and the revised play in one volume). Northwestern University Press Paperback edition published 1986 by arrangement with Grove Press.

Northwestern University Press Paperback Edition published 1986 by Northwestern University Press, Evanston, IL 60201

First Printing

Printed and bound in the United States of America

Library of Congress Catalog Card Number: 86-061247
ISBN: 0-8101-0725-2

Introduction

FACE AND GRIMACE

by Jan Kott

Even the best party becomes a hell if you cannot leave it. Throughout the war in German-occupied Warsaw, a curfew was imposed. An invitation to a party was an all-night invitation. Apartments were small: two, three, rarely four rooms. At each good party there is something of a "happening"— but imagine a happening performed and then repeated with tiresome regularity from 10:00 P.M. till 6:00 A.M. In occupied France a curfew was also enforced. I am pretty sure that Sartre's play *No Exit* originated from the same experience. "Hell is other people." But who am I? I am also somebody else. Guests crowded into a small apartment, drunks among drunks, clearheads among drunks, drunks among clearheads tell themselves their idiotic stories, push themselves into an increasingly grotesque psychodrama from which there is no exit and in which no one plays himself, nor the role that he would choose. He is cast by others. He is cast by the situation. As in the Author's Preface to *The Marriage,* "Being united, people impose upon one another this or that manner of being, speaking, behaving . . . Each person deforms other persons, while being at the same time deformed by them." Rimbaud's "JE est un autre" ("*I* is somebody else") is in Gombrowicz's interpretation a *"gueule"* put on me, and my only recourse is to make an even worse *gueule*—to grimace—an even more horrible and shameful *gueule* on others.

3

Introduction

In the winter of 1943 in occupied Warsaw, I was invited by a young actress to an all-night party. Toward morning, strange sounds reached me from the next room. I opened the door a crack and noticed two young men kneeling opposite each other. They were banging their heads against the floor, and then, at the count of three, they raised their heads and mimicked each other, grimacing in the the most sinister way. It was a duel of grimaces until the opponent had been completely wiped out, until a face was made against which there could be no counter-face. All faces were permissible: intimate and sexual, professional and political, ideological and historical. The face of a virgin, of a queer and of a bridegroom, of a patriot and of a traitor, conservative and radical, Churchill's face and Hitler's face, and finally the face of Father, the face of King, and the face of God. I can't remember any more whether there was an appropriate answer to the face of God. It was already daybreak and I left.

One of the two young men engaged in this duel of grimaces was Jerzy Andrzejewski, the other Czesław Miłosz. Andrzejewski, author of *Ashes and Diamonds,* is one of the most outstanding writers living in Poland. Miłosz's *The Captive Mind* is among the most important books published in the 1950's.

It is not so important that it was specifically these two writers who knelt opposite each other and made horrible faces that winter night of 1943—but even then they were both possessed by Gombrowicz. Not only these two. Already there were a few of us who had been infected by Gombrowicz, or more precisely by *Ferdydurke.*

"The two contestants will stand facing each other and will make a series of faces. Each and every constructive and beautiful face made by Siphon will be answered by an ugly and destructive counter-face made by Mientus. The faces made will be as personal and as wounding as possible, and the contestants will continue to make them until a final decision is reached."

4

He fell silent. Siphon and Mientus took up their positions. Siphon tapped his cheeks, Mientus rolled his jaw, and Bobek, with his teeth chattering, said:

"You may begin!"

At these words reality burst from its frame, unreality turned into nightmare, the whole improbable adventure became a dream in which I was imprisoned with no possibility of even struggling. It was as if after long training a point had been reached at which one lost one's own face. It would not have been surprising if Mientus and Siphon had taken their faces in their hands and thrown them at each other; nothing would have been surprising. I muttered:

"Take pity on your faces, take pity on my face, for a face is not an object but a subject, a subject, a subject!"

Ferdydurke was published in Poland in 1937. In this novel we have the whole Gombrowicz. It is still his most important book. Out of the duel of grimaces in *Ferdydurke* later developed the Gombrowiczian theory of social behavior and particularly of aggression and mutual debasement. This duel contains Gombrowicz's entire theater. What is more theatrical than this carnival game of exchanging masks? And what could be more Molière? Obviously this Moliéresque Gombrowicz or Gombrowiczian Molière (Gombrowicz was always for me more in the tradition of Molière than of Shakespeare) is perfidious and turned around. But, in fact, not so remote from modern interpretations of Molière as it might seem. Moliéristes, even the most dignified among them, have recently become more and more concerned with the problem of face and mask.

Tartuffe is a mask, but does a true face of Tartuffe exist? He is not what he pretends to be and what he pretends to be is someone else. He performs, but what happens if he performs faultlessly? He pretends, but what happens if he pretends perfectly? He wears a mask, but what if he never takes it off? A perfect impostor is a living contradiction. He has become his role. He no longer has a face; the mask is his face. Tartuffe is a fake saint. But the fake saint is the true Tartuffe. Tartuffe plays: lies and pretense are his truth *as an actor.* "The falsest of appearances joins the truest being . . . The result is . . . that in order 'to be true' the actor must *play false.*" I quote from Sartre, from his Introduction to Genet's *"The Maids" and "Deathwatch"*; we are close to the ambivalence of modern theater.

Molière's Tartuffe is not a perfect impostor. He plays badly. He overacts. His mask falls off. Tartuffe is not just a hypocrite, a *faux dévot,* he is an *apparent* hypocrite, a *faux faux dévot.* Hypocrisy is already a role—that is, a fake; a false hypocrite is a role on top of a role, a face on a face, impurity on impurity. Pure Gombrowicz! "Their truth is their lie," writes Sartre about *The Maids,* "and their lie is their truth." A final quotation, "Once again the fake is true and the true can be expressed only by means of the fake."

In his Preface to *The Marriage,* Gombrowicz writes: "The characters in this play do not express themselves directly; they are artificial; they are always acting. The play is thus a waterfall of masks, gestures, shouts, grimaces . . . It should be played 'artificially,' but never at the expense of the normal human quality that is discernible throughout the text."

The mask falls off for the first time; Damis secretly observes Tartuffe's seduction of Elmire and tries, unsuccessfully, to tell everything to Orgon. Tartuffe kneels. He confesses his guilt. He makes a face on a face, truth on a lie, which is a new lie.

> TARTUFFE: . . . Do you think, my brother, that I am what I look like? Because of what people see me do, am I a better man? No, no, you are taken in by appearances. I am, alas, nothing like what people think I am. They

all take me for a good man, but the complete truth is
I'm worthless.*

And now Orgon is on his knees. For each pious contortion
of Tartuffe, a pious contortion of Orgon. He will surrender
everything, if only Tartuffe remains. The two fat men now
kneel opposite each other and distort their faces in foxy
grimaces. The devout face of Tartuffe is countered by the even
more devout face of Orgon, and this in turn by the super-face
of Tartuffe. Tartuffe and Orgon engage in a duel of grimaces,
humility and dignity, like Siphon and Mientus in *Ferdydurke:*

> [Siphon] burst into tears, pious, bitter tears, floods of
> tears, that reached the heights of remorse, revelation, and
> ecstasy. Mientus burst into tears too, and sobbed and
> sobbed until a tear trickled down to the end of his nose—
> whereupon he caused it to drop into a spittoon, thus
> reaching a new level of disgustingness. This assault upon
> the most sacred feelings was too much for Siphon . . . [he]
> beat a hasty retreat, recomposed his features, and once
> more elevated his eyes towards heaven. He advanced one
> foot slightly, slightly ruffled his hair, caused a lock to
> droop over his forehead, and froze into a position of un-
> shakeable unity with his principles and ideals; then he
> raised one hand, and pointed towards the stars. This was
> a powerful blow.

Ultimately, who puts a face on whom in Molière? Tartuffe on Orgon or Orgon on Tartuffe? All Tartuffe's grimaces
are for the benefit of Orgon. Orgon is his audience. For
Orgon he lies prostrate in church, casts his eyes to heaven,
and lasciviously distorts his face when Dorine appears to him
with bared breasts. In Gombrowicz's anthropology, *cul,* back-
side, butt, the pink fanny of the baby, and *gueule,* face, grimace, mug, are key concepts. In Gombrowicz's system, the back-

---

* *Tartuffe,* IV, 6, in Will G. Moore, *Molière: A New Criticism* (New
York: Anchor Books, 1962).

side and the *gueule* are as important as in Sartre, "en soi et pour soi." However, this pink bottom and mug (*pupa* and *gęba* in Polish) are much more palpable, physical, concrete. Tartuffe's faces, all his holy faces, serve to bring about Orgon's final "bottomification." Of all comic characters, Orgon is the most perfect embodiment of Gombrowicz's infantile cruelty, fanny-pink and soft-fresh. Orgon is necessary for Tartuffe, but Tartuffe is even more necessary to Orgon. Without Tartuffe, Orgon, Père Orgon, could never become Père Ubu. Tartuffe is his raison d'être, his philosophy and justification. If there were no Tartuffe, Orgon would have to invent him. For Orgon, Tartuffe is God, but for himself, he preserves the role of king. Without a God in the house, he could never have become a domestic tyrant.* Orgon and Tartuffe are created by and for each other. Each alone is incomplete, unfinished, in the Gombrowiczian sense, immature. Tartuffe is a starving cheat, Orgon a frustrated tyrant. Each needs a grimace from the other. They ascend on each other's faces. However, their imagined patterns and models, that of a perfect hypocrite and a family tyrant, are also inadequate, unsuccessful, and apparent. Authenticity does not arise from faces only. When the Sun King (the real King is a *rex ex machina* for a happy ending and consequently also a fake) orders Tartuffe to be led out under guard, Orgon will remain alone. All his faces have fallen off; he has no face at all.

"Le monde n'est composé que des mines," wrote La Rochefoucauld in his *Maximes*. During my first year at Yale, I lived in the guest suite in one of the colleges. Every Friday there was a mixer. At five o'clock chartered girls arrived, tightly packed in chartered buses. In the buses they had changed from girls to Dates. They had the smiles of dates,

---

* Lionel Gossman, *Men and Masks: A Study of Molière* (Baltimore: Johns Hopkins Press, 1963). "Orgon is bent on using Tartuffe as much as Tartuffe is bent on using him . . . Orgon sets himself up against society as the only true Christian in it. The function of Tartuffe is to guarantee Orgon's superiority to everybody else."

voices of dates, hairdos of dates, panties of dates, and bras of dates. They brought sex along with them, putting on sex like sweaters and bell-bottomed pants because dates must be sexy. The boys were no longer boys. They lost all their charm, simplicity, and freshness; grimacing, they reacted to the artificial female faces with even more artificial male faces. In mutual degradation and imposing their fanny-pink maturity on each other, the boys and girls practiced the obligatory ritual of Friday dating. Till two o'clock in the morning the mixer lasts with terrifying American punctuality and precision. Everything planned in advance—coffee, drinks, dinner, dancing, petting, and the good-night kiss.

La Rochefoucauld said: "The world is composed entirely of grimaces." Gombrowicz reverses this sentence; the grimace is the first and material reality of the world. Each ceremony, ritual, and initiation, which in his terminology he calls "Form," is a Face. Form originates from mutual deformation, imposing on each other female-male faces, adult-immature faces, faces of the Son, of the King, and of God. Form arises from debasement.

Gombrowicz, like Genet, and others, is fascinated by ceremony. As in Genet, theater is ritual, but ritual performed and repeated on stage. Thus, ritual is at the same time a counter-ritual, an aping of ceremony, therefore a repetition of faces by actors. In this mutual distortion and mockery, the actors create their social roles. To be somebody means for Gombrowicz to be inflated by the form, and therefore deformed. To be somebody is to be somebody or something else, inauthentic.

In *The Marriage,* Gombrowicz uses the logic of nightmare. Dreaming, we are ourselves and not ourselves. We are ourselves because we dream. We are not ourselves or we are not fully ourselves because we are dreamed. Our body is also limited, concentrated in one part: arm, leg, member. It is a deformed corporality. We are lighter or heavier. Our freedom of movement is restricted. We cannot get out of our own

9

dream. The dream is real, because it is we who dream, but at the same time, the dream is an illusion because it is only a dream. In dreams our relation with others and with our own ego is degraded, immature, compromised. Id has no face. Everyone in the dream gets his face from the dream. The dream is composed only of faces. In his journal Gombrowicz writes: "Is there anything strange in the fact that the dream (which is a discharge of the anxieties of the day) shows to Henry the ruin and degradation of his parents, his fiancée, his home? Is it so strange that in this dream, dreamed in an inn, there appear drunkards, and that these drunkards begin to harass the father when he forbids them to get at Molly? Is it not logical and in harmony with the situation that the father, mad with fright, proclaims himself—to escape the touch of the drunkards—untouchable king? And that Henry feels that the miracle will be sustained or turned into a farce depending on himself—is this not a feeling we have in many dreams?"*

When the Drunkard in the key scene of *The Marriage* points his erect finger at the Innkeeper-Father, Henry kneels, and by kneeling creates the dignity of the Father and the obedience of the Son. The Father is King, because the King is Father. However, the King is not complete without God. Therefore, the Father of the King is God the Father. The Father now sinks to his knees. They kneel before each other, like Orgon and Tartuffe, like Mientus and Siphon, like Andrzejewski and Miłosz. They kneel and trade grimaces: the face of the Son, the face of the Father, the face of the King, the face of God the Father. As in Molière, Tartuffe conquers in this scene. He assumed the face of God: "In all things let the will of Heaven be done." In *The Marriage*:

> HENRY: . . . (*He gazes around with distrust and kneels down.*) . . . I am kneeling before him and he is kneel-

* *Dziennik* (1957–61) (Paris, 1967), p. 161.

ing before me. This is a farce! What an old copycat
he is! (*With increasing rage.*) How disgusting!
FATHER: Wait a minute! I'm kneeling in the wrong direction. (*Kneels down with his back to* HENRY.) I kneel
down before the Lord! I address myself to the Lord!
I commend myself to Almighty God, to the Holy
Trinity, to His inexhaustible goodness, to His mercy
most holy, His protection most sublime . . .

Now the Innkeeper-Father points his erect finger to
heaven. Like Tartuffe, like Siphon in *Ferdydurke,* like the
Drunkard a moment ago. In Gombrowicz ceremony is parody
of ceremony, ritual, a mockery of ritual. Taking an oath one
raises one's fingers. I raise my fingers and I am somebody else.
"I do," I am king. "I do," I am president. "I do," I am judge.
"I do," I am sworn witness. "I do," I am married. The Innkeeper transformed into Father, Father into King, King into
God the Father, in turn transforms Henry into the Prince; and
Molly, the wench from the inn, sport for the drunkards, becomes the innocent bride. The marriage can now take place.
But before this happens the King-Father will be dethroned,
and Henry himself will proclaim himself King. This role is
also ready-made. The Usurper is King Ubu.

In Gombrowicz's theater, as in Genet's, ceremony is mockery. The Black Mass is an insult to a god in whom one does not
believe. But if there is no God, there can be no blasphemy.
For Genet the impossibility of fulfillment, the grimace before
the mirror, the gesture in empty space or in a locked cell is
tragic. For Gombrowicz this absolute impossibility is grotesque. Gombrowicz's theater is more vulgar, physical, and
coarse. Siphon's erect finger, the Drunkard's huge finger which
he points at the Father, the King's finger raised upwards—
each has its glaring phallic imagery. Gombrowicz is close to
del arte, the farce, and Molière, and what is probably more
striking, to young American playwrights.

The American motel also has its liturgy and ceremony:

silence, order, and respect for civilization are required in it. It is for married couples; they must sign the guest register. Purity, sanity, and morality are guarded by the proprietor.

In Jean-Claude van Itallie's play, *America Hurrah,* a huge puppet with a vacuum cleaner stands on the threshold of the room. She is waiting for the American couple. They arrive. He and she. Two puppets. They close the door and methodically, systematically with American precision, they demolish everything in the room. They tear comforters and sheets, break the armchairs, smash the television set, pull out the shower in the bathroom. They write obscenities on the walls, draw female-male genitals. Then they tumble into the unmade bed.

For this theater, Gombrowicz is a forerunner. He is fascinated by degradation, destruction, debasement, and by all that is shameful, low, and physical, things that are natural and therefore called unnatural. The attempt to rebuild order and bring about the solemn ceremony of marriage is degraded and destroyed by universal stupidity and aggressiveness, personified by the chorus of Drunkards shouting, "Pig! Pig!" This need for shame and artificiality is clearest in Gombrowicz's attitude to Woman. Before becoming the bride the girl must be debased, must be a wench in the inn, must lose her virginity, to have this "virginity" artificially restored by ceremony. As in the case of Genet, Woman becomes sexually arousing only when mated with masculinity, when she has been part of another man, when another man is still fresh in her. The girl in the girl must be destroyed, must be made to resemble the farmhand as much as possible.

HENRY: All the same, who knows whether it is possible . . . whether in general it is possible for a man to fall in love with a woman without the co-operation, without the intermediary of another man? It may be that in general man is incapable of responding to woman

12

except through the intermediary of another man. Might this not be some new form of love? Before, only two were needed, but today it's three.

The Marriage ends in catastrophe. Just as remnants of day pass through dreams, the most nonrealistic work contains fragments of reality, a sphere of meaning which can be explained directly and simply.

The Marriage could take place anywhere or nowhere at all, but this particular Henry begins to dream in France. The hero not only has a name, he is a Polish soldier during World War II. We can even set the action precisely—in June of 1940 after the defeat of France near Dunkirk, where the routed Polish units desperately awaited evacuation to England. A return to Poland was impossible for years. For more complex reasons, personal and political, the return to Poland seemed impossible for the émigré Gombrowicz when in 1946, in Buenos Aires, he was writing *The Marriage*. The Poland that he had left in 1939 no longer existed. This *impossible* return to a *real* Poland is transformed in his dream into a *possible* return to an *unreal* Poland. As Poland becomes more artificial and anachronistic, the more *real* becomes the return. And so, the manor and the inn, the relics of old country life, and finally the feudal archetypes of King, Prince, and Usurper. It is certainly not accidental that Act III of *The Marriage*, showing the grotesque cruelty in Henry's reign, is like *Ubu Roi* in its texture and atmosphere. As in *The Marriage*, the action of *Ubu Roi* takes place "in Poland, that is, nowhere." However, even in fiction and dream, this return to the most unreal of homes and the most unreal of marriages cannot be fulfilled.

The Marriage ends with a funeral march and Henry imprisoned. As in Genet's *The Maids*, Solange and Claire can only kill Madame in a symbolic ritual gesture. To kill or sleep with her they have to *play* her. In reality, the poor maids sleep together or poison each other. The pressure of reality is stronger than any fiction, and the only *real* return to Poland that Gombrowicz could imagine was a return to prison.

In 1942 after the defeat of France, in the most hopeless of the wartime winters, the drunken night parties in Warsaw sometimes ended in a duel of grimaces from *Ferdydurke*. But this game could not change anything; it was only a grimace at a blacked-out window, beyond which spread the night of occupation. *The Marriage* has a bitter taste, Polish and universal.

Translated by L. KRZYZANOWSKI

Author's Preface

IDEA OF THE PLAY

Man is subject to that which is created "between" individuals, and has no other divinity but that which springs from other people.

This is exactly what is meant by that "earthly church" which appears to Henry in his dream. Here, human beings are bound together in certain forms of Pain, Fear, Ridicule, or Mystery, in unforeseen melodies and rhythms, in absurd relations and situations, and, submitting to these forms, are created by what they themselves have created. In this earthly church the human spirit worships the interhuman spirit.

Henry elevates his father to the dignity of king so his father can bestow the sacrament of marriage upon him, after which he proclaims himself king and seeks to confer the sacrament upon himself. To this end, Henry compels his subjects to invest him with divinity: he aspires to become his own God.

But all of this is accomplished by means of Form. Being united, people impose upon one another this or that manner of being, speaking, behaving . . . Each person deforms other persons, while being at the same time deformed by them.

Hence this play is primarily a play about Form. Here, however, it is not so much a question of selecting the most appropriate form with which to convey some conflict of ideas or persons, as one might expect to find in other plays, but rather of rendering our eternal conflict with Form itself. If in a play by Shakespeare, for instance, someone cried at his father, "You pig!" the dramatic effect would depend upon the fact that a son was insulting his father; but when that occurs in this play, the drama takes place between the person who cries and his own cry. His cry may assume a positive or a negative character; it may exalt the person who uttered it or, on the contrary, it may thrust him into an abyss of shame and disapprobation.

The process of deformation to which above all the principal character Henry is subjected is achieved in two ways:

On the one hand, the external world is deformed by the hero's own internal world: Henry dreams everything, he is "alone." The others are merely a product of his dream and at times their utterances correspond directly to the hero's own state of mind. If, then, for no apparent reason a scene becomes indecent, pathetic, or mysterious, if a character suddenly becomes malicious or depressed, it is due to the intensive laboring of Henry's spirit.

On the other hand, the external world imposes itself upon Henry. As we have said already, there are times when the characters in the play change their tone abruptly and utter something unexpected—because that is precisely what Henry expects them to do. Sometimes, however, it is Henry who behaves in a manner which is unpredictable and which even he is at a loss to comprehend, because he must adapt himself to his partners; it is they who dictate his style.

The process of deformation, therefore, is a reciprocal one, a constant struggle between two forces—one internal, the other external—each imposing limitations upon the other. This type of dual deformation can be applied to every act of artistic creation, and for this reason Henry resembles an artist in a state of inspiration rather than a person who dreams. Everything in the play "creates itself": Henry creates a dream and a dream creates Henry, the action of the play creates itself, people create one another, and the whole pushes forward toward unknown solutions.

From the above, come the following:

Idea of the Play

Instructions with Respect to Acting and Direction

1. The characters in this play do not express themselves directly; they are artificial; they are always acting. The play is thus a waterfall of masks, gestures, shouts, grimaces . . . It should be played "artificially," but never at the expense of the normal human quality that is discernible throughout the text.

There are two elements which lend this artificiality an aspect of genuine tragedy. Henry does not regard his fantasies merely as an idle pastime, but as a real spiritual process taking place within him; he is likewise convinced that his words and actions have in a way been conjured up by some mysterious and menacing powers. He believes that Form is creating him. He is a director.

2. This dual deformation produces something which Witkiewicz* would have called "Pure Form." The characters in this play take pleasure in their performance; they become intoxicated with their own personal suffering: for them everything is merely a pretext for joining together for the sake of this or that effect.

One word leads to another, one situation leads to another. Sometimes a detail becomes exaggerated, or sentences, through repetition, acquire an immeasurable importance. It is important, therefore, that the "musical element" of the play be adequately stressed. Its various themes, crescendos and decrescendos, pauses, sforzandos, tuttis and soli should be executed in precisely the same manner as a symphonic score. The actors should behave like instruments in an orchestra and their gestures should be in accord with their words. Let the scenes and situations flow freely into one another; let the various groups of characters communicate some secret meaning.

By studying the text of a normal play, an actor is usually

---

* Stanislaw Ignacy Witkiewicz (1885–1939), Polish dramatist, philosopher, painter, and novelist.—TRANS.

17

able to infer from the contents how a given line should be delivered. In this play, however, the problem is more complicated: for one thing the dialogue is more artificial, and quite frequently the most pedestrian words are charged with artificiality. Furthermore, the stream of dialogue is more dynamic. If, for example, one character utters something in a soft and wistful tone, another may respond in a powerful and thundering voice, while a third may switch into verse and begin reciting some rhythmical stanza.

3. Just as Henry oscillates between Wisdom and Folly, between Priestliness and Madness, so, too, the play itself is constantly threatened by elements of mediocrity, ridiculousness, and sheer lunacy. This is likewise reflected in the language used by the characters, particularly when they speak in verse. In many instances the play takes on the character of a direct parody of Shakespeare. The décor, costumes, and masks of the actors should all convey that world of eternal artifice, eternal imitation, falsity and mystification.

The Action of the Play in Brief

Act I

Henry, a soldier stationed in France during the last war, sees his house in Poland and his parents in a dream.

The house looks as though it has been converted into an inn, while Henry's parents appear to have been transformed into innkeepers. With difficulty Henry recognizes his fiancée Molly in the person of the servant girl. But along comes the Drunkard at the head of the other Drunkards, and when the Father-Innkeeper stops him from making any passes at Molly, the Drunkard starts to harass him.

Panic-stricken, the Father cries out that he is untouchable. "Untouchable as a king!" reply the Drunkards. Henry, who for some time now has found himself in a highly emotional state, kneels down before his Father and by rendering him homage transforms him into an Untouchable King. This untouchableness makes the Father immune to the Drunkard's "touch" and enables him to escape the other's efforts to harass him.

When Henry's filial piety begins to flag, the Father proposes the following arrangement to him: you acknowledge me as King and I, by my sovereign power, will restore your fiancée's purity and dignity which she forfeited in the inn; I will transform her into an Untouchable Virgin and command that you be given a "respectable" marriage which will make everything pure and holy.

Act II

Preparations are made for Henry's "respectable" marriage with Molly.

But the power of the King is threatened by treason (a conspiracy among the Dignitaries).

Henry is convinced that everything depends on how he regards his dream—whether he regards it "wisely" or "foolishly." He delivers a "wise" speech and thanks to this gains a temporary advantage over the Traitors.

But just as the marriage is about to be conferred, the Drunkard (who has managed to escape from prison) intrudes and with the help of the Traitors renews his attack against the King in an attempt to "touch" him with his magnified Finger.

Henry runs to the aid of his Father and his fiancée. Reality teeters back and forth between "wisdom" and "folly." Vanquished by Henry's "wisdom," the Drunkard seemingly resigns his plan. But in order to achieve his intended aim by yet another means, by subterfuge, the Drunkard suggests a talk with Henry in private.

The scene is afternoon tea. "Help us overthrow this weak

and defenseless King," the Drunkard tempts Henry, "and we will make you King, whereupon you can grant yourself a marriage by your own authority."

Henry, half-drunk, realizes with horror that he has become implicated in the plot; but at the last moment he regains his senses and, while pretending to have accepted the above proposition, provokes a *coup d'état* and has the Drunkard arrested.

But the King-Father is unable to master his fear, his magnified "royal" fear. He begins to fear his own son and this fear transforms Henry into an actual traitor: the son turns against his Father, dethrones him, and proclaims himself King. Now, at last, he has control of the situation! Now, as King, he will grant himself a marriage!

But the Drunkard, by joining Molly and Henry's friend Johnny in an artificial·manner before the eyes of the entire court, plunges the new King into a hell of jealousy.

Act III

Henry's reign is a reign of tyranny. He makes preparations for his marriage. Realizing it is others who transform a man into a higher being endowed with power, even into God, Henry resolves to make his subjects "pump" him full of divinity through tokens of respect and obedience. Only then will he be able to confer a "truly sacred" marriage upon himself, a marriage that will restore purity and virginity to his betrothed.

But jealousy undermines him. His parents, wishing to avenge themselves for their persecution and torture, further enkindle the fire of his suspicions.

Only Johnny's death can restore his strength and peace of mind. But for this death to constitute a definite affirmation of his royal power, it is essential that Johnny kill himself at Henry's behest. Henry proposes the idea to him, even though he realizes it is "not really meant in earnest."

Idea of the Play

At the decisive moment when he is about to confer the marriage, the King, now racked by pangs of conscience and jealousy, begins to yield to the importunities of the Drunkard, who has returned to the offense once again. At this time Johnny's corpse is displayed: his friend has slain himself in order to fulfill Henry's will.

Henry does not know whether all of this is "real" or "unreal." He sees himself in a world of fiction, dream, lies, a world of Form. And yet this world corresponds to some reality, it expresses something.

Oppressed by an act which he committed (Johnny's death) and yet did not commit, an act which issued from him and yet was distinct from him, Henry proclaims he is innocent. But submitting at the same time to the formal logic of the situation, to the pressure of Form which has assigned to him the role of a murderer, Henry orders himself imprisoned.

W. G.

Written in Buenos Aires in 1946, *The Marriage* was first performed in Paris in January, 1964, at the Théâtre Récamier, directed by Jorge Lavelli, scenery and costumes by Krystyna Zachwatowicz, music by Diego Masson. It was awarded the first prize of the Concours des Jeunes Compagnies. The cast was as follows:

FRANK, *father and king*	Alexis Nitzer
KATHARINE, *mother and queen*	Juliette Brac
HENRY, *son and prince*	Olivier Lebeaut
JOHNNY, *friend and courtier*	François Mirante
MOLLY, *servant and princess*	Claudine Raffalli
DRUNKARD	Fernand Berset
CHANCELLOR	Luc Delhumeau
CHAMBERLAIN	
CHIEF OF POLICE	Augy Hayter
BISHOP PANDULF	} André Cazalas
DIGNITARY/TRAITOR	

Dignitaries, Drunkards, Courtiers
Ladies, Henchmen, Lackeys

23

ACT I

An oppressive, forlorn landscape. In the
shadows, ruins of a disfigured church.

HENRY:

The curtain has risen . . . An obscure church . . .
An incongruous ceiling . . . A strange vault . . .
And the sign slips into the abyss of the abyss
Of the sphere of spheres, and stone and stone . . .

Through an entrance that has never been entered
Stands a deformed altar of a foreign Psalter
Clasped shut by the absurdity of the chalice
That sinking into stillness gouges out the pastor. . . .

A void. A desert. Nothing. I am alone here
Alone
Alone

But perhaps I am not alone; who knows what is behind
me, perhaps . . . something . . . someone is standing here
alongside me, off to the side, off to the side, some id—
. . . some insuperable, ungovernable, idiotized, idiotouch-
able idiot, who can touch and . . . (*With alarm.*) I'd
better not move . . . no, don't move, because if we move
. . . he'll move . . . and touch . . . (*With growing uneasiness.*) Oh, if only something or someone would come out
from somewhere, for example somewhere . . . Aha!
There's something . . .

JOHNNY *emerges from the shadows.*

Johnny! It's Johnny!

JOHNNY: Henry!

HENRY:

> Imagine what a horrible dream I had
> I dreamt I saw some hideous monster, and
> I wanted to run, but couldn't!

JOHNNY:

> That stew they give us for supper is pretty
> Tough and indigestible. I have nightmares too
> Sometimes . . .

HENRY: But at least you are of flesh and blood. Or perhaps you're only a dream too. . . . What are you doing here, anyway?

JOHNNY: Search me.

HENRY:

> Johnny, Johnny, why are you so frightfully sad?

JOHNNY:

> And you, why are you so sad?

HENRY:

> No special reason.

JOHNNY:

> No special reason.

HENRY: Something strange has happened to us. Where are we? I'm afraid this place is under a curse . . . and we're under a curse too. . . . Excuse me if my words sound artificial . . . I'm unable to speak naturally . . .

> A hundredfold sorrow
> A grief without cease or limit
> And a terrible oppression, dumb and dark,
> Have invaded my soul! Oh, God!
> Oh, God! Oh, God!

JOHNNY (*petulantly*):

> What do you need God for when I am here?

Don't you see, friend, that I am the same as you?
Why let yourself get upset by ghosts
If you and I are of flesh and blood
If you are as I and I am as you!

HENRY (*joyously*): "If you are as I and I am as you!" Oh, what's the difference! But I'm sure glad you're here, Johnny! With you here it's a different story. But . . . where are we? All the same I have the feeling . . . we're somewhere. . . . There . . . there's something over there . . .

Part of a wall becomes visible, some furniture, the outline of a room.

I've seen all this before somewhere.

JOHNNY: So have I . . .

HENRY (*dramatically*):
We are somewhere
We are somewhere. But where?
What's that?

A room appears—the dining room of a country manor house in Poland that looks as though it has been transformed into a dive.

JOHNNY (*hesitantly*): I swear this room reminds me of something . . . It reminds me a little of your dining room in Maloszyce. It's similar and yet not similar . . . That clock. That chest of drawers. There's the room I slept in when I came to visit you during the holidays . . .

HENRY: Yes, but wait a minute—we're not in Maloszyce . . . we're stationed at the front in northern France—at the front in northern France—at the front in northern France. And if we're here, we can't be there!

JOHNNY: It's similar and yet not similar. . . . It would seem to be the same dining room, even though it does resemble a

27

restaurant or a dive . . . or an inn . . . or a boardinghouse
. . . or a tavern . . .

HENRY: This room is disguised and everything is abnormal.

JOHNNY:
Don't be silly, stop trying to complicate matters.
What do you care if something's abnormal
As long as we are normal!
And these chairs are real, they're made of wood, and
one is sure to find something in the cupboard.
But why isn't anyone here? Hallo!

HENRY (*terrified*): Don't shout! Wait! You'd better not shout!

JOHNNY:
Why shouldn't I shout?
Hallo! Is anybody here? Is everybody dead? Hallo!

HENRY:
Fool! Shut your trap!
Shhh! Be quiet, I say! Hallo!
Why doesn't anybody come out? Shhh! Hallo!
Hallo! Hallo!

JOHNNY: Hallo!

HENRY: Hallo!

JOHNNY: Hallo!

Enter the FATHER, *old, rigid, sclerotic, distrustful* . . .

HENRY: At last, someone . . . Excuse me, is this a restaurant?
(*Silence.*) Is this a restaurant?

FATHER: And what if it is?

HENRY (*in the style of a traveler*):
Tell me, is it possible
To get a bite to eat here?

FATHER (*in the style of an innkeeper*):

28

I guess so
But by shouting you won't get anywhere

HENRY (*to* JOHNNY): That voice sounds familiar.

JOHNNY: He looks very similar to your father. . . . I swear it's him, though on second thought . . . I'm not so sure. . . . It's hard to tell at first sight.

HENRY: You're crazy. If that were my father, he'd be the first to recognize us. No, come on, let's forget about it. That's not my father. Come on, let's sit down. (*To the* FATHER.) Is this an inn? I mean, is it possible to get a room for the night here?

FATHER (*grudgingly*): I guess so, seein' as we rent rooms here. But you gotta be well-mannered . . .

HENRY:
Oh, I see, well-mannered . . .

FATHER (*crescendo*):
Polite and respectful!

HENRY:
Oh, I see, respectful . . .

FATHER (*shouting*):
Civil and courteous!

Enter the MOTHER, *an elderly woman, worn out, dressed in rags. She joins in shouting with the* FATHER.

MOTHER: You'd better behave yourselves, and mind you no hanky-panky, because we won't cater to that around here . . . we want no part of that, no sir. . . . We'll have no part of that! . . .

JOHNNY (*to* HENRY): That's your mother.

HENRY (*loudly*):
It would seem so

29

But it's not altogether certain
This is all a little confusing, but I shall
Straighten everything out!

(*To* JOHNNY.) Forgive me for speaking artificially, but I feel as though I were in an artificial situation. (*Raises the lamp.*)

Come over here
Come over here . . . Come over here, I say

Come closer, that's it, closer! I swear, you'd think I were trying to lure a bunch . . . a bunch of chickens . . .
Keep coming! Closer! Look how grudgingly they come. Come a little closer or else I shall have to come closer.

I'll come closer, and as I come closer

You come closer . . . My God, it's as though I were trying to catch a bunch of fish. But why is it so quiet around here?

My Father has stepped out of the shadows
But he's changed so much
I can hardly recognize him
And moreover so strangely silent that
I must speak the whole time alone
Alone must I speak until I'm transformed
Into a priest of my father!
And here comes my mother like a steamer
To tell the truth she's not very similar to my mother
Perhaps I should just drop the matter. How strange
My voice sounds. Let's leave them alone since
They wish to be left alone.

JOHNNY: Maybe they're not your parents at all.
HENRY:

It's them all right, I know perfectly well it's them
But something's happened to them and for some
reason

30

They're pretending not to be them
Perhaps they've gone crazy . . .

JOHNNY: Try talking to them in a straightforward manner, Henry.

HENRY:

> . . . And I'm unable to speak to them straightfor-
> wardly, because
> There's something very solemn and mysterious about
> all this
> Exactly as though a mass were being celebrated!
> I feel like laughing when I see how solemn I've be-
> come!
> My words sound so dignified! I'm simply amused
> To see how grave and solemn I've become
> But at the very same time I tremble and trembling I
> declare
> That I tremble—and as a result of this declaration
> I tremble even harder and trembling even harder

I again declare that I tremble even harder . . . But to whom do I make this declaration? To whom? Someone is listening to me . . .

> But I don't know who—and as a matter of fact
> I am alone here, all alone, since you are not here
> No! There's no one else here! I am alone
> All alone, completely alone . . . Oh, weep! Yes, shed
> Tears for me, because I am alone, alone, alone!

JOHNNY: Don't say that . . . Why do you say such things?

HENRY: Still, if they are my parents the least I could do is go up to them and say hello . . .

> Father! Mother!
> Papa! Mamma! It's me, Henry!
> I've come home from the war!

FATHER (*reluctantly*):
Mother . . . it's Henry!

MOTHER:
Henry! Good Heavens!

HENRY (*with animation*):
Hey, they said something!

MOTHER: Oh, who could have ever foreseen by a divine premonition that something like this . . . oh, my little treasure, my little sunshine, my little sweet pea, oh, what a silly old woman I am not to have recognized you, oh, how could I have been so blind, and how I used to cry my eyes out for fear I would never see you again, my little sunshine, but here you are, my little sweet pea, my little sparrow, my little treasure, oh, and how you've grown, you're a man now, alleluia, alleluia, come here, let me hug you, my little sweet pea, my little sparrow, my little treasure, my little sunshine, oh, oh, oh . . .

HENRY:
Come, let's hug each other.

MOTHER:
Oh, yes, yes, let's hug each other.

FATHER:
Well, all right, let's hug each other.

MOTHER:
Come, let me hug you.

FATHER: Wait just a minute! Not like that.

HENRY: But it's only mamma!

FATHER: Mamma or no mamma, I wouldn't get too close if I were you.

HENRY: But . . . but I am the son.

FATHER: Son or no son, I wouldn't get too close if I were you.
. . . Maybe you are the son, but there's no telling what
the son has been up to all these years. No sooner does he
set foot inside the door and right away he has to be
hugged. (*Sharply.*) Well, nobody's gonna put his arms
around me, see, 'cuz I ain't no duffel bag you can just
flop down in any corner you feel like!

HENRY (*to* JOHNNY): They've gone crazy.

JOHNNY (*to* HENRY): They've gone crazy.

FATHER: And let's cut out all this buddy-buddy stuff too, 'cuz
once ya start that the next thing ya know some jerk'll
up and pull a fast one on ya, and then whaaam, right in
the kisser . . . or somewhere else for all I know . . . and
then pretty soon they'll be tryin' to take advantage of
ya, shovin' ya all around and (*heavily, sclerotically*)
whackin' ya in the puss, persecutin' the hell out of ya,
houndin' and tormentin' ya, with no regard whatsoever
for age or sex, with their goddamn, pitiless, spiteful
spite . . .

HENRY: They've gone crazy.

JOHNNY: They've gone crazy.

HENRY (*unrestrainedly, emphatically, theatrically*):
It's obvious they couldn't take it
They've lost their wits
After all these long and agonizing years
But such is life. The world nowadays is swarming
With half-wits . . .

JOHNNY (*as above*):
The world is swarming with half-wits. At least
Half of all the mothers and fathers in the world
Have lost their wits because they couldn't endure
Suffering, affliction and disease
I know of many such cases myself.

33

HENRY:
So do I!

(*Falls silent, ashamed.*) Nevertheless, I must try to make a little conversation with them. (*Loudly, in a conventional tone.*) To tell the truth, I didn't recognize you at first.

MOTHER: Neither did we.

HENRY: I didn't recognize you, because . . . well, because I didn't expect . . . But that doesn't matter. It's not of any real importance. So how have you been getting along?

FATHER: Not bad. What about you?

HENRY: All right, I guess.

FATHER: Hm . . .

HENRY: Hm . . .

Silence.

Well, what'll we do now? We can't just stand here and do nothing . . .

FATHER: Nothing.

MOTHER: Nothing.

HENRY: Nothing.

JOHNNY (*unexpectedly*): I could eat something.

MOTHER: But of course! Here we are gabbing away a mile a minute, oh, but of course, what's the matter with me, of course, one has to have a bite to eat, certainly, just a minute . . . I'll have something ready in less than no time, why of course, this is a day to celebrate, because our darling Henry has come home, let's see, we'll find something to eat, just a minute, just a minute . . . Here's a table and here are a few chairs . . . You'll have to settle for potluck, it isn't what you'd call a feast exactly, but it'll have to do, I guess, alleluia, alleluia . . .

FATHER: That's the spirit, mother, fix us something to eat, but in a manner which is fitting, with respect . . . as is proper . . . And so, in the name of the Father and of the Son, of the Mother and of the Son, please be seated at our table, my son . . . But we can't just sit down at the table in any old way . . . The table's over there and we're over here . . . so give me your arm, my son, and you, old girl, let this young gentleman show you to the table, for such is how it has always been in our family for centuries and centuries, amen. And now, forward, march!

HENRY: Very well.

They walk two by two.

MOTHER:
I still can remember how His Reverence the Pastor
Escorted me to all the festivities at Easter
The table would be laid, the guests all engaged
In the most cheerful conversation!

FATHER (*thunderously*):
In those days, gentlemen, a man would sit down
To a freshly laid table, and tuck away his pea soup
With such appetite and zest, one would have thought
He were ringing the bells or blowing a trombone!

JOHNNY:
How pleasant it is to walk and how pleasant
To exclaim words out loud!
But if we all continue to prate
I'm afraid we shall never get anything to eat!

HENRY:
I'm a little confused about this procession of ours. I'm not sure

> Whether I am leading father, or he is leading me
> And the form of our meeting strikes me as queer
> But one must adapt oneself to the general
>   atmosphere . . .

ALL:

> Yes, each must adapt himself to the general atmosphere!
> Each must adapt himself to the other! Then a concert
> will erupt!

HENRY: How extraordinary!

They sit down at the table.

MOTHER: Forgive us for offering you such a modest meal, Henry, and you too, Johnny . . . but you see, we do the best we can under the circumstances. This is a soup made from horse guts and cat piss.

FATHER: Be quiet, woman! What difference does it make what it's made from. You've probably noticed, Henry, that you've found us in a somewhat embarrassing situation in this dumpy, dumpable dump of a roadside dump —well, you see, that's because there was a storm, a snowstorm, the roads were closed, not a soul, thunder and lightning, puddles of water, mud everywhere. . . . Keep your spoon where it is, son, your father hasn't lifted his spoon to his mouth yet.

HENRY: This tavern . . . it reminds me of something.

FATHER: Never mind about that, forget about it.

MOTHER: There isn't any.

JOHNNY: No.

HENRY: Nothing.

FATHER: It's been transformed.

MOTHER: Distorted.

JOHNNY: Destroyed.

HENRY: Dislocated.

All right, all right, they *have* gone crazy. But they couldn't have gone crazy, because they don't exist and I am only dreaming . . . and the surest sign they don't exist is that I'm able to say they don't exist right in front of them. They only exist in my head. Oh, my head! I've been talking to myself the whole time!

JOHNNY: How's that? What do you mean you've been talking to yourself the whole time?

HENRY: Oh, skip it! (*He begins to eat.*)

FATHER: Keep your spoon where it is—your father still hasn't lifted his to his mouth yet.

HENRY: Father, mother—how oppressive all these dreams are— father, mother—as if I didn't have enough problems of my own—father, mother—and all this time I thought they were dead—but not only are they not dead, they are sitting here and . . .

FATHER: You are a faithful and devoted son, and consequently you will not wish to commence eating before he who has sired you . . .

HENRY: And I won't go back to my family. I don't have a family any more. I am no longer a son.

FATHER (*as though he were preaching a sermon*): Gone forever is that love and fidelity which the son has always owed the father, because for centuries and centuries, amen, the father has always been a hallowed and sacrosanct saint, an object of filial devotion under the pain of eternal chastisement . . .

HENRY: I am a son of the war!

The Marriage

FATHER: And whoever raised a sacrilegious hand against his father would commit a crime so appalling, so unnatural, so abominable, so monstrous that afterwards he would pass the rest of his days, from one generation to the next, amid screams and groans of anguish, as one condemned by God and by Nature, heaped with shame, abandoned, accursed, rejected, forsaken, tormented . . .

HENRY: The old man's afraid I might belt him . . .

FATHER: Good soup.

HENRY (*to* JOHNNY): Think you could lick this father?

JOHNNY: If you could, I could.

FATHER: Pass me the salt.

HENRY: And you wouldn't feel any pangs of conscience afterwards?

JOHNNY: I would if I were alone, but not if there were the two of us, because one would imitate the other.

FATHER: Nothin' I like better than stuffin' my gut with tripe.

HENRY (*to* JOHNNY): Har, har, har! Well said, Johnny, well said. I agree with what you said just now—har, har, har, yes, yes, I agree with you one hundred per cent. But that's beside the point. (*With growing anxiety.*) No, that's completely beside the point. That's not what I had in mind at all. Oh, the hell with it! I'll be damned if I know what's going on around here! All I know is that this is all frightfully oppressive, because everything is twisted, understand, bunged up, plugged up, yes, that's it, plugged up . . . and disguised . . . but it seems as if we're not the only ones here. . . . I would like to penetrate, elucidate, to solve the riddle . . . (*He turns the lamp into the center of the room, revealing* MOLLY, *who is asleep in a chair.*) Who is that girl?

MOTHER: Oh, that's the girl who does the service around here.

HENRY: Service?

MOTHER: That's right, a maidservant . . . she serves as a maid.
. . . Molly, bring us those scraps and that cat cutlet that
are lying on the window sill. . . .

The FATHER *scratches himself.*

Are you itching again?

HENRY: By the way, as long as we're going on about nothing
in particular . . . Are any of our friends still alive?

FATHER: A few.

HENRY: Tell me something, I'd be curious to know . . . whatever became of Mary, you remember, the girl I was once
engaged to . . . the one who used to come here for the
holidays . . .

FATHER: I don't see any cutlet.

MOTHER: Maybe somebody swiped it.

MOLLY (*comes closer*): It's not on the window.

MOTHER: Go look in the reception room, but no dilly-dallying,
mind you. . . . Clear the dishes away first.

HENRY: What's your name?

MOLLY: Molly.

FATHER (*in an ambiguous tone*): Molly.

MOTHER (*as above*): Molly.

FATHER:
    She's a servant girl . . . She serves . . .

MOTHER:
    We hired her . . . for everything . . .

FATHER:

> She's an all-round servant.

MOTHER:

> She serves the guests.

FATHER:

> She serves to render service . . .
> Molly

MOTHER: Molly . . .

FATHER: Molly . . .

HENRY (*to* JOHNNY, *quietly, sadly*): What do you think about all this?

JOHNNY (*quietly, helplessly*): I don't know . . . I don't know . . .

HENRY (*to* JOHNNY): No, but I know!

JOHNNY (*to* HENRY): If that's her, why doesn't she speak up? . . . She couldn't have forgotten us. . . . Say something to her, Henry.

HENRY:

> No.
> How can I speak to her if
> She no longer exists
> She used to exist . . .
> Oh, what a dirty trick!
> I once had a noble father and mother
> And a fiancée as well, but now it appears
> My father has shut himself up in some inexplicable
>   tower
> My mother has become equivocal
> And my fiancée has been swallowed up by a slut
> Bunged, beaten and plugged up by a slut
> And forever imprisoned in a slut . . .
> Oh, what a dirty trick!

How vile! How base! How vulgar! But the worst thing
   of all is
I couldn't give a damn . . . Hear
With what ease I say that: I couldn't give a damn.

JOHNNY (*lightly*): Neither could I.

HENRY (*lightly*):
   To tell the truth,
   I don't have the faintest idea
   How I should behave:
   The girl I was once engaged to has now become a slut.

JOHNNY: What of it?

HENRY:
   What of it?
   Exactly—what of it—since
   All of this is just a mere detail.

JOHNNY:
   A detail!
   Millions of girls
   Have suffered the same fate.

HENRY:
   Exactly!
   Millions of other people
   Are in the same situation as I.

JOHNNY: The world over!

HENRY: In Warsaw and Peking!

JOHNNY: In Verona and Barcelona!

HENRY: In Paris and in Venice!

JOHNNY: In Liverpool and Istanbul!

MOTHER: In Lyons and in Toulons!

FATHER: In Bucharest and Budapest!

JOHNNY: In Dublin and Berlin!

HENRY: Come on, let's dance!

ALL (*suddenly*): Let's dance!

HENRY:

>The son has returned to the house of his parents
>But the house is no longer the house
>And the son is no longer the son. So who
>Has returned and to what?
>Let's forget about the past! Let's march forward!
>May no one return to anything!

Quiet.

Here is where I sat with her, and once again I'm sitting here. But what difference does it make? It's all over now. Finished. There's something else now and there'll be something else again tomorrow. It's not worth repeating.

Quiet.

JOHNNY: It's not worth repeating!

HENRY (*in a romantic tone*):

>Do you see this chair here? That's where I sat with her
>On that memorable night! This is where
>My mother sat and my father over there!
>Exactly as I'm sitting here now. Do you remember?
>That memorable night, our last night together?

MOTHER: Of course I do, my child, of course I remember. . . . I sat right over here, and we had sour milk for supper . . .

FATHER: I sat over here.

JOHNNY: And I sat here . . . here, in this chair, because I remember I was looking out the window and I said: "There are flies here." It all comes back to me now!

HENRY: And I sat over here . . . (*He sits down.*) I was buttering

my bread, with her beside me here . . . I was buttering my
bread. (*To* JOHNNY.) Why don't you sit down? Sit down.
I was buttering my bread.

    And I said: Schearing
    Has inquired about that syringe again.

FATHER: I said something, but I can't remember what.

MOTHER: You don't have a very good memory, but I do. . . .
Now what was it you said? Oh, yes! You said, "My
sleeve" . . . nothing else, just "my sleeve," because he'd
just got his sleeve caught against the salad dish.

FATHER: That's it! That's it! That's it! I said, "My sleeve," on
my word of honor! What an extraordinary memory you
have!

HENRY: And then I started drumming my fingers on the table
and I said: "I'm getting married in three months."

MOTHER: That's just what he said, my little sparrow, that's
exactly what he said, those are the exact same words he
used, that's just how he put it. And then I laid down my
cup, chased away another fly and said: "Henry, what's the
matter with you? What's that you're saying? Are you
engaged? But isn't that a little . . ." No, I've got it all
wrong. First I said: "Henry, darling, what are you saying?
. . . Pass me the sugar."

FATHER: That's right, that's right, and then I said: "Let them
be happy, mother! Now, now, no need to cry. Bring us
something to drink! You're both a little young, but
never mind that." And did she ever blush! Turned red
as a tomato! Well, I never! Har, har, har!

MOTHER: And then she said something.

HENRY:
    Yes, she said something, but she's gone now.

The wedding fell through. Finished. Nothing.
There she is, hiding in the closet! She refuses to come
out.
Oh, what's the use! I'm surrounded by a void. And all
she does is pout.
Forward! Forward!

ALL (*except* MOLLY): Forward!

FATHER: The hell with it, shit and goddamit!

HENRY (*to* JOHNNY): How do you like that—a common ordinary
maidservant!

JOHNNY: Well, so what if she's a maidservant?

HENRY: That's right, so what if she's a maidservant.

JOHNNY: She's not even bad-looking.

HENRY: You're right, she's not bad-looking, at that.

JOHNNY: Does she sleep here?

HENRY: Does she sleep here?

JOHNNY (*playfully*): I would like some tea. (*To* MOLLY.)
Psssst . . . Psssst . . .

FATHER: What's all this psssst-psssst for? There's no need to
psssst around here. If you want something else, all you
have to do is ask me. And don't think you can get away
with anything, 'cuz we're not running some dive here,
you know . . . Ohoh, did ya see that? They're already
givin' her the eye! Christ almighty, it's always the same,
night or day, someone's always trying to pinch her, pat
her, cuddle her, fondle her, tickle her crotch, and it
always winds up in trouble, trouble, trouble . . . (*Sharply.*)
Don't try to cause any trouble, I'm warning you guys!

MOTHER (*in a shrill voice*): Frankie!

FATHER: Don't start anything, I'm warning you!

Act I

MOTHER: Calm down, Frankie!

FATHER: Kindly keep your piggish paws off this swinish sow of a pigged-up pig of a swineherder's pig prick!

MOTHER: Look at him slobber!

FATHER: Pig, pig, pig!

The DRUNKARD staggers in.

DRUNKARD: Porky Molly!

FATHER: Get outta here!

DRUNKARD: Hey, Molly, how's 'bout a li'l piece of pork, eh?

FATHER: I'll get it for you myself.

HENRY (*on the other side, amused*): Porky Molly!

FATHER (*running up to him*): I'll serve it to him!

DRUNKARD: Hey, Molly, gimme some pork!

HENRY (*obstinately*):
        Porky Molly!

DRUNKARD:
        Gimme some pork, Molly!

HENRY:
        Porky Molly!

FATHER:
        Oh, for chrissakes!

DRUNKARD:
        Pig!

HENRY (*yelling into space*):
        Pig!

JOHNNY:
        Pig!

45

MOTHER (*aside*):
Heaven help us—what a pig!

FATHER (*to the* DRUNKARD):
Get outta here!

DRUNKARD:
A bottle of bitters!

FATHER (*to* HENRY):
Get outta here!

HENRY:
A bottle of bitters!

DRUNKARD (*louder*):
A bottle of bitters!

HENRY (*louder*):
A bottle of bitters!

FATHER:
Good God!

DRUNKARD:
A bottle of pig bitters!

HENRY: A bottle of pig bitters!

JOHNNY: A bottle of pig bitters!

The DRUNKARDS *come in.*

DRUNKARDS:
Chug, chug, chug!

FATHER:
Gentlemen, be reasonable!
It's almost closing time. Molly, lock the doors!

The DRUNKARDS *sit down at the table.*

DRUNKARDS:
Some English stout!

46

A pint!
Some headcheese!
A double shot, straight!
Molly, some English stout! Molly, some kielbasa! Molly,
    some sausage!
Molly, some headcheese!

HENRY (*aside*):
    Molly, some headcheese!

DRUNKARDS:
    Maxie's a good-humor man
    Hits the bottle when he can
    Chug, chug, chug!

FATHER (*to* MOLLY): Hey . . . don't wait on that table!

DRUNKARD: Ah, come on, Molly, come on over here for a
    second, I wanna tell you something, Molly baby . . .

FATHER: Don't go, Molly.

DRUNKARD: Aaaah, shut your lousy trap, grandpa. . . . If I feel
    like callin' the waitress she ain't got no right to refuse,
    goddamit, and if you try to get tough with me, ya old
    coot, I'll blow myself up and blow off your crucifix!

HENRY (*aside*): Blow off his crucifix!

FATHER: Wait a minute, wait a minute! Okay, okay—Molly,
    go wait on that table!

DRUNKARD (*looking at him*):
    He has the runs.

DRUNKARDS (*matter-of-factly*):
        He has the runs.

HENRY (*aside*):
            He has the runs.

DRUNKARD:
    Shaaat up . . .

47

> Close ranks! March!
> Forward! Let's go!

A furious march.

DRUNKARDS:

> *Maxie's a good-humor man*
> *Hits the bottle when he can*
> *Chug, chug, chug!*

They stop in front of the FATHER.

DRUNKARD:

> Shut your traaap . . . you pig . . .
> Pig!
> He has the runs . . .
> That's what's the matter, he has the runs like crazy
> He's gone and shit his pants!

2D DRUNKARD (*gloomily*):

> He has the runs.

3D DRUNKARD:

> Has he ever . . .

DRUNKARD: And seein' as he's scared shitless of me, I'm gonna let 'im have it. Ain't that right, Miss Molly?

DRUNKARDS:

> Well, let 'im have it then! Let 'im have it!

DRUNKARD:

> I'm gonna let 'im have it!

DRUNKARDS:

> Well, let 'im have it then! Let 'im have it!

DRUNKARD:

> I'm gonna let 'im have it!

HENRY:

> Well, let 'im have it, let 'im have it!

Act I

DRUNKARD:
> I'm gonna let 'im have it!

MOTHER (*in a shrill voice*): Frankie, they're going to let you have it!

DRUNKARDS:
> All right, boys, let's let 'im have it!

DRUNKARD:
> All right, let's let 'im have it!

They advance toward the FATHER.

DRUNKARDS:
> All right, let 'im have it!

DRUNKARD:
> I'm gonna let 'im have it!

Silence.

> I'd let 'im have it, but the son-of-a-bitchin'-son-of-a-bitch has a kisser like a rock . . .
> It won't budge . . . And if it won't budge, then . . .
> (*To* MOLLY.) Molly!
> There's a lot of room on the floor!

DRUNKARDS (*sullenly*): It won't budge . . . (*To* MOLLY.) Molly . . .

DRUNKARD: And that's not all . . . Look how quiet it's become . . .

HENRY (*to himself, aloud*): It's true. It has become quiet in here . . .

DRUNKARD: Chug, chug, chug!

A furious march.

DRUNKARDS:
> *Maxie's a good-humor man*

49

Hits the bottle when he can
Chug, chug, chug!

Well, let 'im have it!

DRUNKARD:

Okay, I'm gonna let 'im have it!

HENRY (*to himself*): How much longer can this go on?

DRUNKARD (*aside, in a different tone*): Not much longer now.

HENRY (*to the* DRUNKARD): What's outside the window?

DRUNKARD (*as above*): Fields—as far as the eye can see.

The DRUNKARDS *approach the* FATHER.

But first of all I'm gonna paste this guy right square in
the kisser, and then I'm gonna stomp on him, flatten him,
squish out his guts and spit all over 'im 'cuz I ain't afraid
—Molly . . .

But he's got a mug like a rock!
And if it won't budge, there's not a damn thing I can
do . . .
But what a mug he's got, what a mug!

2D DRUNKARD:

A mug like a house!

3D DRUNKARD:

A mug like a priest!

Silence.

4TH DRUNKARD (*suddenly*): Hey, he's got a fly on his nose!

DRUNKARD: So what?

4TH DRUNKARD: Well, why don't you knock it off for him?
You're not gonna just let it sit there, are you? Ain't that
right, Miss Molly?

Act I

DRUNKARD: Godammettydamndamn fly, godammettydamndamn
fly, godammettydamndamn fly . . . (*He raises his hand.*)

FATHER (*very softly*): Don't you dare . . .

HENRY (*aside, dramatically*): Oh, oh, he said something!

FATHER (*softly*):
Don't you dare, I won't tolerate it
I won't tolerate it
I won't stand for it
I won't stand for it, because I won't stand for it
I can't stand it!
And if I can't stand it, then . . . then . . .
Then I don't know what . . .

DRUNKARD (*confidentially*):
I'm gonna let 'im have it, Molly, I'm gonna let 'im
have it!

DRUNKARDS (*confidentially*):
Well, let 'im have it then, let 'im have it!

FATHER (*shouting*):
You pigs!
Keep away from me, or you'll be sorry
If anybody touches me, something awful
I repeat: something awful
So awful that . . . that I don't know what.
There'll be weeping and screaming and the gnashing
of teeth,
The rack and execution, hell and execration,
A leveling, piercing, pulverizing squeal
That'll blow this whole universe to kingdom come . . .
Indeed! Indeed!
Because no one, because no one may touch me
Because no one, because no, be-be-because
I'm untouchable, I'm untouchable, I'm untouchable
Because I'll curse the lot of you!

DRUNKARDS:
>Tut, tut, tut! A king, a king, an untouchable king!

DRUNKARD:
>Get a load of this guy! He's a king!
>Just for that I'm gonna touch him with this finger!
>Ain't that right, Miss Molly?

FATHER (*fleeing*): Keep away from me, or I'll curse you!

HENRY (*suddenly*): Stop! Stay where you are!

>*The stage becomes motionless.*

>I really don't know how I ought to behave . . . (*To* JOHNNY.) Johnny! But I suppose I shall have to behave somehow or other . . . (*With regret.*) Forgive me for speaking in an artificial manner, but everything here is artificial!

JOHNNY (*briskly, defiantly*):
>Don't worry about it!
>What do you care if something is artificial
>As long as you yourself are natural!

HENRY:
>That's right, I am natural, I would like to be natural
>I don't want to be solemn! But how can I help
>Not being solemn when my voice sounds solemn?

>*Silence.*

>What a terrifying silence.
>It's so quiet my ears are ringing
>And how strange, how awfully
>Strange that I am speaking
>But if I were silent
>My silence would likewise seem strange
>What am I to do?
>Suppose I sat down

In this chair here
>   (*He sits down.*)
>   and started
Cracking jokes, laughing, or moving
My hands and feet . . . No, it's no use! Even
The artlessness of these gestures is artificial
And they are transformed into some sort of spell . . .

Suppose I put my feet up on this table, tossed back my head, lighted up a cigarette and said: What business is it of mine whether they beat up my father or rape my ex-fiancée? . . . What's the sense of blowing everything out of proportion?

Let's not exaggerate!

What's one more or less. . . . Can't he stand it? But I can stand it that he can't stand it. . . . Father, father . . .

What kind of a father is he anyway? He's an ordinary
>   father
The most ordinary kind of father . . . We are all
The most ordinary kind of people . . . Suppose I say
All this and even more. Very well. I said it
But this again
Sounds solemn, and transforms what I am saying into a
DECLARATION
And it sinks like a stone
Into that silence . . . Aha! Now I know why
I do not speak but declare. Because you are not here
And I am alone, alone, alone. I am not speaking
To anyone and therefore I must be artificial
Because if I am not speaking to anyone and yet I speak
>   just the same
Then I must be artificial.

What'll I do? Sit down? No. Go for a walk? That wouldn't make any sense either. But I can't go on behaving as though I had nothing to do with all this. What's a person supposed to do in such a situation? I might kneel down, that's true, I might kneel down. . . . Of course that would be pretty . . . but I did say I might kneel down . . . even though it would look a little . . . but I did say I might kneel down . . .

He kneels down a little on one side.

Well, what do you know! I knelt down. But I knelt down quietly and not for myself, but for them, and not for them, but for myself as though I were a priest . . . a priest . . . of what I don't know . . .

FATHER (*abruptly, aside*): Of what I don't know.

MOTHER: Nobody knows.

DRUNKARD: There's nobody here.

JOHNNY: Nobody, nothing.

HENRY:

It doesn't matter!
I am kneeling here before him! And now try
To dismiss my genuflection, now try to
Ignore my genuflection, now try to make it
Disappear! (*To the* DRUNKARD.) Go on, hit him!
I kneel down before him!

2D DRUNKARD: The King!

MOTHER: The King!

DRUNKARD: The King!

DRUNKARDS: The King! The King!

HENRY: What do you mean, the King?

DRUNKARDS (*completely drunk*):

The King, the King, the King!

Act I

*Their cries become more and more accelerated in tempo.
The* DIGNITARIES *come in.*

FATHER:
> Henry!
> Oh, oh, Henry!

MOTHER:
> Oh, Henry!

DIGNITARIES:
> Henry!

HENRY:
> Oh, Henry! (*Stands up.*)

FATHER:
> Thank you, my son, I accept the homage which you
>   have rendered me
> I accept it and once again I accept it
> And I cannot accept it enough . . .
> (*With sincerity.*) Long have I thirsted after honors.

HENRY: What kind of a masquerade is this?

> *Quiet.*

FATHER (*with difficulty, vehemently*):
> Dignitaries!

DIGNITARIES:
> The King! The King!

FATHER:
> Dignitaries of my Person!

DIGNITARIES:
> The King! The King!

FATHER:
> Dignitaries of my dignity! Bid welcome to the Prince
> Bow down before him in humble obeisance,

Prince Henry, my son, who from a far-off war
Has come.

HENRY: What kind of rubbish is this?

FATHER (*gravely, sclerotically*):
Help! Help!

Oh, sweet Jesus of Nazareth! Oh, Mary most holy! Oh, Jesus, my Jesus! Help me! But it was he, my son, my seed, my offspring most holy who only a moment ago delivered me from

This sow of a souse who, in his drunken stupor,
Blindly, brazenly, with extreme wantonness,
Rushed at me and with
His
Piggish
Finger

My untouchable person tried to touch! My person! My person! My untouch . . . Nobody may touch . . . because it's forbidden . . . Prohibited. Nobody!

DIGNITARIES: Oh, sweet Jesus!

FATHER:
But he won't try to touch me any more!
Nor inflate himself to deflate my person
Nor squish, nor stomp, nor spit on me!
Because Henry, Henry, Henry! Oh, Henry!

MOTHER (*triumphantly*):
Henry!

DIGNITARIES:
Oh, Henry!

HENRY:
Oh, Henry!
This is getting sillier by the minute!

56

FATHER:
> Kneel down
> Kneel down, Henry!

HENRY: What for?

MOTHER (*in a shrill voice*): Kneel down, Henry!

FATHER:
> Kneel down, kneel down! I'll kneel down too
> Kneel down! Let everyone kneel . . . (*He kneels.*)

The DIGNITARIES *kneel down.*

HENRY: I'm not going to stand here by myself . . . (*He gazes around with distrust and kneels down.*) I wish to hell I knew what was going on. (*He notices that he and his* FATHER *are kneeling opposite one another.*) I am kneeling before him and he is kneeling before me. This is a farce! What an old copycat he is! (*With increasing rage.*) How disgusting!

FATHER: Wait a minute! I'm kneeling in the wrong direction. (*Kneels down with his back to* HENRY.) I kneel down before the Lord! I address myself to the Lord! I commend myself to Almighty God, to the Holy Trinity, to His inexhaustible goodness, to His mercy most holy, His protection most sublime . . . Oh, Henry, Henry! . . . In Him is there shelter, in Him is there comfort, in Him is our refuge . . .

> My Father
> Thy son am I
> Thou art my Father . . .

HENRY: He's praying.

FATHER:
> Thou art my king!

HENRY: I can't get up now—it wouldn't be proper.

FATHER:

> Oh, my Father, oh, my King, to Thee I do solemnly
> swear
> Love
> Honor
> Respect

HENRY: He's swearing to God, but it's as if *I* were swearing
to *him*. (*Aloud.*) I've had about all I can take of this.
(*Stands up.*)

FATHER: Henry, Henry . . . My Father, I stand beside Thee,
I am Thy servant. I shall not forsake Thee, my Father,
and in return Thou shalt . . . Thou shalt return my
beloved to me, my sweetheart, amen, amen, amen . . . so
that everything may be done in a respectable manner,
as is fitting . . .

HENRY: Say, what is this? Is he whispering to God or to me?

FATHER:

> Thou shalt return my betrothed to me!

HENRY: He will return my betrothed to me?

FATHER:

> Thou shalt grant me a marriage!

HENRY: He will grant me a marriage?

FATHER: Thou shalt grant me a respectable marriage . . . a
proper marriage as has always been the custom in our
family. . . . As it was in former times! Let everything
be as it used to be! Thou shalt grant me a marriage to
this chaste and immaculate virgin, my fiancée, my sweetheart . . . a respectable marriage . . .

Everyone slowly rises.

HENRY: A marriage?
FATHER: A marriage.

MOTHER:	A marriage.	
HENRY:	A marriage?	
FATHER:	A marriage.	
MOLLY:	A marriage.	
A DIGNITARY:	A marriage.	
MOTHER:	A marriage.	
A DIGNITARY:	A marriage.	
HENRY:	A marriage?	

The FATHER *and* MOTHER *smile at him indulgently, with delight, with emotion.*

FATHER:

> In the name of the Father
> And of the Son! Do you see
> This young lady here who in appearance
> Is nothing but an ordinary maidservant?
> The maidservant of some dumpy dump?

DIGNITARIES: We see her, Sire.

FATHER (*emphatically, insistently*):

> This girl is neither a whore
> Nor a maidservant! She is a noble,
> Modest, untouchable young lady who has been
> Ravished, enslaved, tortured, plugged up,
> Abused and spat upon by these good-for-nothing
> > bums . . .
> In defiance of all laws, human and divine . . . Damn
> > you pigs!
> This girl is not a pig! Have
> A little heart, you people! A little understanding!
> Have a little pity! Therefore I do declare
> And I decree, I command with all my might, I declare
> > once and for all,
> To all those present
> That I restore her former dignity
> And command that she be honored

As though she were myself or the Most Holy
Virgin in her untouchable honor, in the name
Of the Father and of the Son!

HENRY (*to* JOHNNY): This is nothing but a dream, it's only
a dream . . . a little naïve maybe, but what do I care.

JOHNNY: That's right! What do you care whether or not it's
a dream . . . as long as it gives you pleasure.

HENRY: Pleasure.

Meanwhile, the FATHER, MOTHER, MOLLY *and the* DIGNI-
TARIES *gather around him.*

MOTHER: Oh, look how he's blushing!

FATHER: Har, har, har! He's ashamed. . . . Now, now, Henry,
look at me, look at me . . .

HENRY: What for?

FATHER: Because tomorrow's the wedding . . .

HENRY: But I don't understand . . .

FATHER (aside): Tsssst . . . Surely you're not going to fool
around with some cheap two-bit whore, not when you
have the chance to marry a respectable young lady. . . .
In our family it has always been the custom to have a
respectable marriage. Your mother and I were married in
a proper manner, and it is only fitting that you do the
same. . . . You'll see, everything will turn out all right
. . . (*In a loud voice.*) Thank you, my son, for showing
me your affection. . . . Soon we shall be celebrating your
marriage and with it my joy and that of your mother, my
spouse, and as for that which is already past, squandered
and forgotten, we simply won't talk about that any more,
as far as we're concerned it never happened, it no longer
is, it isn't . . .

MOTHER (*in a very loud voice*): Alleluia!

Act I

Music, wedding march. FATHER *and* MOTHER, HENRY *and* MOLLY, JOHNNY *and the* DIGNITARIES *march around the stage in a solemn and cordial procession.*

HENRY (*in a very loud voice*):
> Is it possible to imagine anything more improbable
> Than this farcical march of phantoms in a fog of illusion?
> And yet does it fill my breast with glee and cause my poor heart to sing
> When me to my former lover this festive march does bring.
> (*To everyone.*) Forgive me, I am a rhymester.

MOTHER:
> It's such times as these that gladden a mother's heart,
> Which for so many years has stood in disregard!

FATHER:
> The music is playing, the couples in procession
> As once was the custom in times gone by!
> Follow me, gentlemen! As God is our Protector!
> Don't stop, gentlemen! Come on!
> March forward! Forward! Come on, let's go!
> Faster, faster! Keep in step!
> Step lively, gentlemen! March in style!
> Don't fall behind! March forward!
> Forward! Forward! Come on, let's go!
> (*He notices the* DRUNKARD.)
> Stop, stop, stop! He's come here to gawk at us!
> Seize this man, arrest him and throw him into
> Some dark and dreary, foul and fetid, godforsaken dungeon!
> (*To the* DRUNKARD.) I'm gonna let ya have it, see!

DRUNKARD:
> I'm gonna let ya have it, see!

61

FATHER:
>You?
>Me?

DRUNKARD:
>I'm gonna touch you yet . . .
>(*To* MOLLY.) Ain't that right, Miss Molly?

FATHER: You pig!

DRUNKARD: You pig!

FATHER: You pig!

ACT II

A large room, in semi-darkness.

HENRY *(leaning up against a column)*:
O to divine
The sense of this dream . . .

Two by two the DIGNITARIES *pass by in the penumbra and mount the stairs to an elevated platform which fades away in the darkness.*

1ST DIGNITARY:
A maidservant who served to render service!

2D DIGNITARY:
And the king of the tavern is a tangible tavern-keeper!

They pass by.

3D DIGNITARY:
The wedding will take place shortly.

4TH DIGNITARY:
The wedding? That's a joke!

They pass by.

5TH DIGNITARY: How much longer must we go on making asses of ourselves, poking our noses into this serviceable servant girl's business?

6TH DIGNITARY: And that drunkard has broken loose from his shackles and is roaming about the neighborhood.

They pass by. The FATHER *approaches.*

63

HENRY: Father!

FATHER: Yeah, it's me, Henry . . . They're getting ready for the marriage. In a minute we're gonna give you a wedding that'll make everybody green with envy. . . . (*Pointing into the darkness.*) They're making preparations over there now. Just keep a firm grip on yourself!

HENRY: What kind of a marriage? Who will perform the ceremony, where and how?

FATHER: Who? The Bishop. I've sent for the Bishop to make sure everything goes the way it should. Don't worry. I've taken care of everything, but don't lose your head, Henry, don't lose your head . . . and for God's sake don't do anything stupid—otherwise the marriage will be a flop. . . . Remember, it's not just your father who's involved here—there's your sweetheart to consider too . . .

HENRY (*into space*): Sometimes I think this is all very wise, and other times . . .

FATHER: Tssst . . . But whatever you do, Henry, don't betray me, because there are enough traitors around here already. . . . Don't try to make a laughingstock out of me, Henry, I beg of you . . . because the place is crawling with traitors . . . traitors . . . traitors . . . Traitors! (*He withdraws, then climbs up to the platform.*)

HENRY: I don't know what my feelings are!

Light. FATHER *appears on the platform surrounded by a* COUNCIL AND COURT. *The faces of the* DIGNITARIES *are expressive to the point of caricature, wise, slightly contemptuous; the costumes are magnificent but border on the burlesque.*

What majesty! (*He goes before the throne.*)
Here I am!

Act II

FATHER: Henry!

COUNCIL AND COURT: Oh, Henry!

HENRY: Oh, Henry!

FATHER:
>Henry, my son, we are about to embark
>Upon your nuptial ceremony. Soon
>Will the bridal party usher in the maid
>With whom you'll be united world without end
>Amen, amen.

MOTHER (*fervently*):
>Amen.

CHANCELLOR (*wisely and venerably*):
>Amen.
>That was a grave and lofty speech.

DIGNITARY / TRAITOR (*aside*):
>Amen.
>That was an asinine and ridiculous speech.

FATHER (*as though frightened*):
>I say

It will take place immediately. In a moment. Because it must take place, I decreed it, I proclaimed it . . . And if anybody tries to stand in the way! . . . Out, out, you filthy maggots, out, out, you good-for-nothing bums!

>Oh, oh, gentlemen of my council! A short while ago
>A pack of these slimy, rotten, low-down,
>Stinking, slobbering, soused-up sows
>Attacked me and tried to touch
>My person!

COUNCIL AND COURT:
>Oh, my God!

FATHER:
> Even though I am the King!

COUNCIL AND COURT:
> Oh, my God!

FATHER:
> Even though I am untouchable!

COUNCIL AND COURT:
> For heaven's sake!

FATHER (*heavily, sclerotically*): Oh, woe, woe! What a terrible sacrilege, what an intolerable, unthinkable, unpardonable blasphemy! And that's not all. I hear that sow of a souse has broken loose from his shackles while his guards were out getting pickled. . . . Chancellor of my Council, command that the gates be closed and have the guards put on alert—there's no telling what these drunks will do. I have an itch. Command that the gates be closed!

DIGNITARY/TRAITOR (*unexpectedly, brazenly*):
> Har, har, har! That's impossible!
> Har, har, har!

TRAITORS: Har, har, har!

FATHER: What do you mean?

DIGNITARY/TRAITOR: Forgive me, Your Majesty, forgive me, Your Majesty, but His Majesty can't just close his gates to any old drunk who happens to come along, since that would mean His Majesty is afraid of any old drunk and that would be unthinkable because that would constitute an affront to His Majesty, and His Majesty cannot commit an affront to the majesty of His Majesty . . .

TRAITORS: Well said!

FATHER:
> What, what, what?

I only mentioned it because that drunken swine has been getting more aggressive lately . . . but if it's impossible, then it's impossible. Don't stretch your luck, you pigs! I know what you've got up your sleeves!

> I have no need of such measures
> Because this ceremony will be so ceremonious
> So dignified, so respectable and so majestic
> In all its majestical majesty, that
> No scum on earth would have the nerve to . . . (*Intoxi-cated.*) Sound the trumpets
> Because the son for the greater glory of his father
> Is about to enter the marital state
> By virtue of my royal decree, yes
> By my most sovereign decree
> Now on with it, on with it!
> Come on, let's go!

COUNCIL AND COURT (*standing up with fury*):
> On with it! On with it!
> Come on, let's go!

FATHER: Stop, stop, everything must be arranged beforehand, so everything goes the way it should. . . . I have an itch. Chancellor of my Council, scratch me. Where is the ceremonial cloak? Put the ceremonial cloak and grand-ducal hat on my son and gird him with the sacred sword!

2D DIGNITARY: Amen.

3D DIGNITARY: That was wise.

DIGNITARY/TRAITOR (*aside*): That was silly as a goose!

2D DIGNITARY: Our noble young man will look powerful and magnificent in these vestments.

DIGNITARY/TRAITOR: Comical and idiotic, but that's his affair.

Pause.

HENRY: Do I really have to put all that on? (JOHNNY *hands him the vestments.*) Oh, is that you, Johnny?

JOHNNY: It's me.

HENRY: Who are you, that is to say, what are you?

JOHNNY (*clumsily, as though embarrassed*): I've been assigned to your service, Your . . . Your Highness . . .

HENRY: I can't talk to you. I feel awkward. . . . Hand me my hat. I look funny, huh?

JOHNNY: Yes and no.

HENRY: Now gird me with the sacred sword. This is a joke, but it doesn't matter. The main thing is I'm going to marry her. (*Suddenly this dialogue becomes public, as though both had forgotten about the presence of the* KING *and* COURT.)

JOHNNY:

Of course it doesn't matter
The main thing is you're going to marry her.

HENRY:

I have to adapt myself to the circumstances, but don't
think for a moment
That I take any of this nonsense seriously.
I do it more out of curiosity, I'm anxious to see
What the outcome will be, besides what harm can it
do me
To amuse myself . . .

JOHNNY:

That's the spirit
It's better to amuse yourself
Than to be bored . . .

HENRY: That's it exactly!

Act II

HENRY *turns to the* KING *in his ceremonial attire; laughter of the* TRAITORS; *derisory names are flung down at him.*

1ST TRAITOR: Clown!

2D TRAITOR: Buffoon!

3D TRAITOR: Imbecile!

FATHER (*in a vulgar manner*):
> Aaaah, shaat up!
> Keep your lousy traps shut!
> I didn't give anyone permission to speak!
> I give the floor to my son
> Let him speak. (*Panic-stricken.*) Henreee, say
>   something!

HENRY: What'll I say?

FATHER (*in absolute terror*): Henreee, say something, but for the love of God, say something clever . . . say something clever! Shaaat up, pigs! Now you're going to see how my son can talk . . . he'll put you in your places, he'll teach you a thing or two. Come on, Henreee, say something, but something clever, say something clever, because if you don't then . . . then . . .

HENRY: Then what?

FATHER: That's just what they're waiting for!

General expectation.

DIGNITARY/TRAITOR: He will speak foolishly, because he looks foolish.

2D DIGNITARY: He will speak cleverly, because he looks clever.

General expectation.

HENRY:
> Honestly

69

I don't know what to say, but I shall soon find out
What I will have said.

1st GROUP: What a brilliant idea!

2D GROUP: What an idiotic idea!

HENRY (*musingly*):
I am foolish
And yet I am to speak cleverly . . .

ALL: Here comes a confession . . .

HENRY (*with sincerity*):
Again do my words
Acquire extraordinary power, while I stand here by
myself
And speak to you alone. But what should I say?

(*To himself.*) If I say something wise, it will sound foolish, because I am foolish. And if I say something foolish . . .

FATHER: No, no, Henreee!

HENRY (*to himself*): If I'm unable to uphold the grandeur of
this majesty, this majesty will sink to the level of my
buffoonery. I can't think of anything clever to say—just
the same old empty thoughts and words. . . . Wait a
minute! Now I know what I will say.

(*To everyone.*) My words are vapid
But they reverberate off you
And become magnified by your majesty—
Not by the majesty of the one who speaks
But by the majesty of the one who listens.

1st GROUP:
Well spoken!
Wisely spoken!

Act II

HENRY:

    I am talking nonsense
    But you are listening wisely to me, and hence
    I am becoming wise.

COUNCIL AND COURT: Wisdom! Wisdom!

MOTHER: What a mind he has, eh?

HENRY:

    I have no dignity
    I lost my dignity a long time ago. But my father
    Has elevated me to a new dignity now. And so I'm
        becoming
    Wiser and more dignified than I am. And I accept it,
    Yes, I accept it. I do hereby proclaim
    That I wish to be married in a manner sublime.
    So let's get on with it! Where is she?
    Show her in and forward, forward!

COUNCIL AND COURT (*standing up, with fury*):
    Wisdom! Dignity! Marriage! On with it!
    Forward, forward, forward!

FATHER (*thunderously*): With wisdom profound and dignity sublime has my son expounded. Open the gates and bring in the bride and His Holiness the Bishop, and let the trumpets trumpet with all their might into the very heart of nature; let the trumpets trumpet, I say, so as to terrify and terrorize any pig who's piggish enough to pig up the works, because there's no dearth of these dirty pigs and . . . aaah, the pigggs, the piggggs, the piggggggs . . .

Trumpets. MOLLY, *dressed in a sumptuous gown, comes in together with the* BRIDAL PARTY; *through another door enters* BISHOP PANDULF *followed by his* RETINUE.

FATHER: Henreee!

71

COUNCIL AND COURT: Oh, Henry!

HENRY: Oh, Henry!

FATHER (*in a choked voice, as though frightened*): We are about to begin. . . . In our family it has always been the custom to have a respectable marriage. Don't cry, mother. (*To* MOLLY *and* HENRY.) All right, both of you stand over here . . . bow your heads . . . (*Aloud.*) We are about to embark upon the most holy act of matrimony, in the name of the Father and of the Son . . . (*Aside.*) Kneel down and let the trumpets trumpet. . . . Let the brides-maids take the train in their hands. . . . Chancellor, hand me my scepter . . . put on my crown . . . (*Aloud.*) In the name of the Father and of the Son. (*Aside.*) And now His Holiness the Bishop will bind their hands with the holy sash as proof of this

> Crushing, shattering,
> Omnipotent act performed
> In the presence of our majesty! Sound the trumpets!
> Hand us the holy sash! Down on your knees!
> Oh, Lord! Help! My good people!
> So be it! And so it shall be! Such is my decree!
> Such is my will!

DIGNITARY/TRAITOR (*loudly, insolently*): Treason!

The DRUNKARD *staggers in.*

FATHER (*stupidly*): Heyyy . . . what's going on here?

A long silence.

DRUNKARD: I beg your pardon. . . . It's nothing . . . I was just . . .

FATHER (*terrified*): Ask this man who gave him permission to come in here and have him removed at once.

Act II

DRUNKARD: A bottle of vodka, a fifth, some gin, four bottles of beer and a herring sandwich!

A VOICE: He's drunk . . .

2D VOICE: To the gills . . .

General laughter, sighs of relief.

HENRY:
> I do not know this man, and yet
> I have the feeling I do know him . . .
> (*With solemn meekness.*)
> But in any case
> I cannot help knowing
> Everything which is happening here . . .

FATHER:
> He's drunk . . .
> Throw him out, take him away, show him the door . . .

CHANCELLOR (*approaches the* DRUNKARD): What are you doing here, my good man? Do you not realize that you are standing in the presence of His Royal Majesty?

DRUNKARD: Ai-yai-yai . . . His Majesty the King! Good heavens!

FATHER:
> All right, all right, that'll do,
> You are in luck, my good fellow, you have seen the King
> Now go on home and sleep it off.
> Oh, how distressing is this disease of drink
> That brings our people closer to the brink!

COURT: Oh, indeed! Indeed!

CHANCELLOR: Here, buy yourself a drink, now scram! . . . Why don't you go away?

The following utterances should be pronounced with an air of perfunctoriness, apathy.

73

DIGNITARY/TRAITOR: Why don't you go away?

DRUNKARD: Because I can't.

2D DIGNITARY: You can't?

DRUNKARD: I can't.

3D DIGNITARY: And why can't you?

DRUNKARD: Because I feel funny.

CHANCELLOR (*to the* FATHER):
> The poor fellow's embarrassed, he can't move
> He doesn't know how to behave, har, har, har!

FATHER:
> Har, har, har!

CHANCELLOR:
> Har, har, har!
> (*Indicating the door with his finger.*)
> Beat it, I tell you!

DRUNKARD (*with awe*):
> A finnger!

CHANCELLOR:
> Beat it!

DRUNKARD:
> A finnger!

CHANCELLOR:
> Out!

DRUNKARD:
> What a finnger!

COURT:
> Har, har, har, a finnger, a finnger!

74

Act II

DRUNKARD (*examining his finger*): It's not like mine. . . . Mine is vulgar, grubby-looking . . . a domestic finnger, a peasant's finnger . . . just right for nose-picking.

Laughter.

A coarse finnger, the finnger of a village clod . . . why it's an insult even to dishplay such a finnger before such august personages . . .

CHANCELLOR: Get out of here!

DRUNKARD: Okay, okay, I'm going, but I can't because everyone's staring at my finnger.

DIGNITARY/TRAITOR: Why don't you stick it in your pocket?

VOICES:
Stick it in your ear!
Or stick it in your eye!

DRUNKARD: I'd like to put it away, but I can't, because everyone's looking at it! If I so much as point at something with this finger (*inadvertently points at* HENRY) then right away everybody looks to see what it is I'm pointing at.

HENRY (*softly*):
Pig . . .

DRUNKARD (*softly*):
Pig . . .

(*Aloud.*) They're gawking at my finnger as it if were somehow extraordinary! And the more they look, the more extraordinary it becomes, and the more extraordinary it becomes, the more they look, and the more they look, the more extraordinary it becomes, and the more extraordinary it becomes, the more they look, and the more they look, the more Extraordinary it becomes . . .

75

This is an extraordinary finnger!
This is a powerful Finnger!
Oh, how they've pumped up my finnger!

And if I now decided to . . . to toushhh someone with this finnger . . .

FATHER: Shut up!

DRUNKARD: —even though that person is untoushhable . . .

FATHER: Shut up!

DRUNKARD (*brutally*): And once I toushh, I get cocky!

TRAITORS: Go ahead! On with it! On with it!

FATHER (*shouting*): Pig!

DRUNKARD (*shouting*): Pig!

FATHER (*in a very calm voice*):
  Friends, gentlemen of my Council and personages
  Of my person . . .
  (*He bursts out.*) Hold on to me, I'm exploding!
  (*Frightened by his own outburst.*) I'm bursting . . .
    I'm exploding . . .
  I'm bursting out in such horrifying,
  Terrifying anger, that . . . oh . . . oh . . . oh . . .
  (*Feebly.*) I feel weak . . .

MOTHER: Frankie! He feels weak!

COURT: The King feels weak! The King is sick!

FATHER (*feebly, imploringly*):
  Henreee . . .

COUNCIL AND COURT (*powerfully*):
  Oh, Henry!

HENRY: Oh, Henry!

Act II

Henry, in the name of the Father, in the name of the
   Son
In the name of the Father and of the Son!

HENRY *approaches the* DRUNKARD *whose finger has been dominating the scene.*

   You pig!

DRUNKARD: You pig!

HENRY (*calmly*):
   You pig!
   Put that finger away!

DRUNKARD (*drunk*): I don't know what you're talking about!

HENRY: Put it away, or else I'll put it away for you!

DRUNKARD: A bottle of booze!

HENRY: Put it away or I'll pounce on it and put it away myself . . . I'll pounce on it . . .
      (*A moment later.*) Look how idiotically it sticks out
   . . . right in the middle of everything. . . . No, I can't
   pounce on it . . . because the whole thing is preposterous
   . . . it's too silly for words . . .

TRAITORS (*sharply*):
   Silly!
   Silly as a goose!

HENRY: Stop, stop! I'm not silly—it's that finger which is silly!
   He stuck it out on purpose so as to make a mockery of
   everything—to make me out to be a lunatic!

DRUNKARD (*pointing at* HENRY): Lunatic!

TRAITORS: Lunatic!

HENRY: Be careful, I'm warning you. . . . Don't exasperate
   me, or I shall wake up . . . and you will all disappear . . .
   (*To* MOLLY.) You too will disappear . . .

77

The Marriage

Silence. The stage becomes motionless.

But perhaps
This is not a dream, perhaps I really have gone crazy

Perhaps I'm not here at all, but in reality I'm lying in some hospital, and while feverishly thrashing about, I only imagine that I am here. . . . Who knows what might have happened to me?

Perhaps my brain has been damaged by a bullet?
Or by an explosion?
Perhaps I've been taken captive and tortured, or perhaps
I fell on something, or something fell on me
Perhaps I became bored . . . and was no longer able . . .

Or perhaps they ordered me—dispatched me—forced me to do something which I couldn't bear. No, there is not a single thing which might not have happened to me—everything and even more than everything is possible. But suppose I am not in a hospital and nothing abnormal has happened to me. All right . . . and yet . . . Oh, how many insanities have I taken part in?

Ohhh . . .
Even though I was the most healthy . . . the most
    rational
The most balanced person
Others forced me to commit
Atrocious acts, murderous acts,
Insane, moronic, and yes, licentious acts . . .

This raises a simple question: If in the course of several years a person fulfills the function of a madman, is he not then really a madman? And what does it matter that I am healthy if my actions are sick—eh, Johnny? But those who forced me to commit these insanities were also healthy

And sensible
And balanced . . . Friends, companions, brothers—so
   much
Health
And such sick behavior? So much sanity
And yet so much madness? So much humanity

And yet so much inhumanity? And what does it matter
if taken separately each of us is lucid, sensible, balanced,
when altogether we are nothing but a gigantic madman
who furiously

Writhes about, screams, bellows and blindly
Rushes forward, overstepping his own bounds
Ripping himself out of himself . . . Our madness
Is outside ourselves, out there . . . There, there, out
   there.
Where I myself end, there begins
My wantonness . . . And even though I live in peace
Within myself, still do I wander outside myself
And in dark, wild spaces and nocturnal places
Surrender myself to some unbounded chaos!

CHANCELLOR: This is a funeral march!

FATHER: This is a funeral march!

HENRY:
That's it, a funeral march!
Once again they have spoken. And I have spoken,
And this finger is jutting out in the middle like the
   finger of a lunatic
And here I am talking to myself and gesticulating in
   absolute solitude like a lunatic . . .

DRUNKARD: Lunatic!

TRAITORS: Lunatic!

They advance toward HENRY.

79

HENRY: Stay where you are! I am here at the King's behest.

DRUNKARD: The King is a lunatic!

HENRY:
> Stop!

> Suppose my father has gone mad, but in his madness he is still a defender of virtue and dignity—in which case he can't be mad!

> Yes, that's the truth, that's the most truthful truth—and hence that solemnity, wisdom, and gravity which have descended upon me. Look how wisely I am standing! My wisdom and my dignity are invincible! And he just stands there with his finger like an imbecile!

> Go ahead—I dare you to touch me!

FATHER:
> Henry!

COUNCIL AND COURT:
> Oh, Henry!

HENRY:
> Oh, Henry! . . .
> Throw that drunkard out of here!

The DIGNITARIES *advance toward the* DRUNKARD.

DRUNKARD *(slowly, putting his finger away)*: Hey, not so rough, eh? . . . I'm an intelligent person too . . . (*He suddenly becomes exceedingly clever. To* HENRY.)

> I'm not half
> As dumb as you think . . .

> (*A moment later.*) What d'ya say you and I have a little talk on the side, eh? You know—one wise man to another . . .

HENRY *(startled)*: What about?

Act II

DRUNKARD: We'll see. We'll have a wise little chat . . . (*To everyone.*) Because I'm a wise man, too . . .

HENRY (*hesitantly*):
No. Although . . .
If he wants to talk wisely . . .

DIGNITARY/TRAITOR (*provokingly*):
If he wants to talk wisely . . .

COURT (*somnolently*):
If
if
wisely . . .

HENRY: Very well!

Afternoon tea. LACKEYS *bring in coffee and pastries. The* DIGNITARIES *break up into groups. The* LADIES *fan themselves with enormous fans.*

COURT:
How pleasant it is at His Majesty's tea
To carry on a flirt in a form so discreet
Oh, the toupees and décolletés do the senses arouse
While His Majesty himself does the honors of the house!

May I offer you some pastries? That's very kind of you. Oh, what a splendid crowd! I'm terribly sorry. I bow down before you. Oh, what a magnificent gown!

VOICE OF THE FATHER (*upstage*): All right, give me a little tea too!

A LADY (*passing by, to a* DIGNITARY): Who is that strange-looking character talking with the Crown Prince?

A DIGNITARY: He's a foreign envoy or else an ambassador.

HENRY: All right, give me a little tea too. (*To the* DRUNKARD.) May I offer you some pastry?

DRUNKARD: That's very kind of you. I hope nobody is listening.

HENRY: As you can see, they're going out of their way to make this little chat possible . . . in absolute secrecy . . .

They both walk over to one side of the stage.

DRUNKARD: Well, I'll come straight to the point. . . . I'm not quite as drunk as I appear to be . . . and all these antics of mine are part of a plot to undermine the authority of the King. Many of the dignitaries are conspiring against him, and it was they who dragged me out of prison by the scruff of the neck. But Your Highness spoke just now with such wisdom that . . .

HENRY:
He's trying to flatter me . . .

DRUNKARD: . . . that all my efforts were for nothing. There was only one thing in all this wisdom which struck me as being not quite so wise. . . . Do you believe in God, Your Highness?

HENRY (*into space*):
Since he has asked, I have to say no.

DRUNKARD: Well, then how can you let yourself be married by the King? If God does not exist, how can your father be a king? After all, doesn't his power come from God? And this Bishop is not a bishop on his own power either.

HENRY: I already told you . . . I already answered that. . . . Even if my father were an ordinary madman who only imagined he was King, he is still a defender of virtue and dignity. . . . And even though I do not believe in God, I do believe in Moral Law and Human Dignity on earth.

How solemn I sound!

DRUNKARD: And who established that law if there isn't any God?

HENRY: Who? People.

DRUNKARD: Then why do you wish to make this such a solemn
occasion if it is merely a product of man's imagination
like everything else?

HENRY (*flustered*):
  As a matter of fact
  To a certain extent he's right. I don't believe
  In any of this . . . I behave
  As though I believed in it, and yet I don't believe in it
  I respect it, and yet I don't respect it . . . I genuflect
  But I don't genuflect . . . I humble myself
  And yet I don't humble myself
  And I know that all of this is just a farce. And so
  The greater my wisdom, the greater
  My stupidity . . . Shhh! Shhh! Quiet!
  He mustn't find out about this!

DRUNKARD: Why does Your Highness place him above yourself
if it was you who put him on the throne in the first
place?

HENRY (*to himself*): That's true. And if he is not my King, I
am not his Prince . . .

DRUNKARD: And the same is true of your fiancée. . . . If it
was you who made him King, and if it was the King who
elevated her to the dignity of a virgin, that would mean
it was you, Your Highness, who made a virgin out of her.
. . . And what kind of a virgin is that, I ask you?

HENRY: It was I who made a virgin out of her. This drunkard
has a pretty clear head on his shoulders. . . . And yet

  If it were really that simple, why
  Do I feel as though I were celebrating
  Some sort of elevated mass?

DRUNKARD: A mass?

HENRY: A mass.

DRUNKARD: A mass?

HENRY: A mass.

(*Gravely*.) Get away from me: I am a priest . . .

DRUNKARD (*slowly*): I am a priest too . . .

COURT:

> *Oh, the toupees and décolletés do the senses arouse*
> *While His Majesty himself does the honors of the*
> *house!*

HENRY (*sadly*): He's mimicking me, he's mimicking me so as to make a fool out of me. A moment ago he was talking sense, but now he's talking nonsense . . .

DRUNKARD: Nonsense?

HENRY (*thoughtful*): Nonsense. I thought he was more clever . . .

DRUNKARD: Clever?

HENRY: Clever.

DRUNKARD: Clever?

HENRY: Clever!

DRUNKARD (*exploding*):

> Now I shall tell you something and cleverly, too
> About that religion whose priests we both are. Between
>   ourselves
> And through ourselves is our God born
> And not to heaven, but to earth does our church belong
> We create God and we alone, whence does arise
> That dark and terrestrial, ignorant and bestial
> Intimate and inferior, humanly human mass
> Whose priest I am!

84

Act II

Both PRIESTS *begin making wild and pathetic gestures.*

HENRY:

Whose priest I am?
But . . . I don't understand.

DRUNKARD:

You don't understand
And yet somehow you do understand. You understand
Because I understand.

HENRY:

You understand
Because I understand. You? Me? Which of us
Is speaking and to whom? I don't quite see . . .
No, no, I don't exactly see . . .

DRUNKARD:

Do you see
This finger? (*He shows him his finger.*)

HENRY:

Do you see
This finger? (*He shows him his finger.*)

DRUNKARD:

Yes, I see it
I see that finger!

HENRY:

And I see it too!
Oh, what wisdom, what profundity! It's as though
I were looking at myself in a thousand mirrors!
Your finger, my finger!

DRUNKARD:

My finger, your finger, your finger, my finger! Between
ourselves.
It's between ourselves. Would you like me

85

> To anoint you priest
> With this finger?

HENRY:

> Would you like me
> To anoint you priest
> With this finger?

DRUNKARD:

> Oh, yes, gladly.

HENRY:

> Oh, yes, gladly.

> *The* DRUNKARD *makes as if to touch him.*

> There's that finger again! You pig!

DRUNKARD: You pig!

HENRY: You pig!

> All he ever wants to do is touch me!
> (*Checking himself.*) May I offer you some pastry?

COURT:

> *How pleasant it is at His Majesty's tea*
> *To carry on a flirt in a form so discreet*
> *Oh, the toupees and décolletés do the senses arouse*
> *While His Majesty himself does the honors of the*
> *house!*

HENRY (*to himself*): Oh, I let myself be taken in by words, and all this time he just wanted to touch me. I'd touch this moron who's been trying to make a moron out of me . . . I'd touch him and throw him out, but there are too many lights here, too many women and too many dignitaries. (*He makes for the* DRUNKARD, *but the* DIGNI-TARIES *intervene.*)

DIGNITARY/TRAITOR (*to the* DRUNKARD): My dear Ambassador!

A LADY (*passing by*): Who is that mysterious gentleman who has been chatting with the Crown Prince for such a long time?

A DIGNITARY (*emphatically*): He's a foreign envoy or else an ambassador!

A LADY: An ambassador!

DIGNITARY/TRAITOR: My dear Ambassador!

2D TRAITOR: Dear Mr. Ambassador!

3D TRAITOR: My dearest Ambassador!

DRUNKARD (*eloquently*):
    Ah, greetings, gentlemen, greetings!

A LADY:
    My dearest Ambassador Plenipotentiary!

DRUNKARD:
    I bow down before you, madam.

    Ceremonious bows.

HENRY: Hmmm . . . A few minutes ago he was just a drunkard, and now he's an ambassador. I'd touch him, but I have no desire to make a fool of myself. One has to keep up appearances.

DRUNKARD: Forgive me, ladies and gentlemen, but I would like to have just a few more words with the Crown Prince. Then I shall be completely at your service.

TRAITORS: We shall not disturb you, Your Excellency. (*Deep bows; they withdraw.*)

DRUNKARD (*to* HENRY): This is indeed a magnificent reception!

HENRY: Indeed it is.

COURT:
    Oh, the toupees and décolletés do the senses arouse

87

The Marriage

While His Majesty himself does the honors of the house!

The AMBASSADOR *and the* PRINCE *stroll back and forth with this elegant reception in the background.*

DRUNKARD (*in the style of a diplomat*): In regard to what we were just saying, His Highness will be pleased to observe. . . . Please believe me when I say that albeit I am a foreign ambassador, still do I harbor the most fervent feelings of devotion and respect for the person of His Royal Majesty. On the other hand, I should say it is precisely on account of this feeling of love and respect that I fear . . . or rather, I suspect . . . and to a certain extent even know . . . that many of your eminent dignitaries have of late estranged themselves, so to speak, from the throne . . .

HENRY (*diplomatically*): Is that so?

DRUNKARD: As a sincere friend and devoted servant of the royal family I consider it well-nigh my duty to apprise Your Highness of this state of affairs in a confidential manner.

HENRY: I am extremely indebted to you, Mr. Ambassador.

DRUNKARD: There is no question, Your Highness, but that your father is a great monarch, or so it would seem to me at least . . . but it is not at all inconceivable, I am afraid, that his concept of power is not altogether consistent with the spirit of modern times.

DIGNITARY/TRAITOR: You could not have couched it any better, Mr. Ambassador.

DRUNKARD: That he is a grand and imposing figure cannot be disputed, but the anachronism of his concepts is all too evident—an anachronism, I might add, which is peculiar to persons more advanced in years. (*In a confidential manner.*) But, really, Your Highness—to believe in some code of morality and decency that has been laid down once and for all? Between you and me, modern man must be exceedingly more flexible; modern man knows that there is nothing permanent or absolute, but that everything is forever creating itself anew . . . creating itself between individuals . . . creating itself . . .

HENRY: One cannot deny that you are a flexible person and that you are constantly creating yourself anew . . .

DRUNKARD: Looking at it objectively. . . . But let's have something to drink, eh? To His Majesty's health!

DIGNITARY/TRAITOR: To His Majesty's health!

HENRY: To His Majesty's health!

DRUNKARD: Let's see, what were we talking about? . . . Ah, yes. . . . It is for that very reason that not a few of the dignitaries have, so to say, estranged themselves. . . . Har, har, har, but His Majesty's greatest enemy is yourself, Your Highness . . .

HENRY: Me?

DRUNKARD: Har, har, har! Because the admiration which your noble qualities arouse . . .

HENRY: He's trying to flatter me . . .

DRUNKARD (*in a confidential manner*): Many people here believe you are the one who ought to be in power. . . . But let's have something to drink, eh Prince? To His Majesty's health!

DIGNITARY/TRAITOR: To His Majesty's health! Many people here have no other desire—after a very long life for His Majesty—save that of seeing you in power . . .

DRUNKARD: And then His Highness could grant himself a marriage . . . or even do without a marriage altogether, har, har, har—instead of submitting to these old-fashioned ceremonies!

DIGNITARY/TRAITOR: Let's have another glass! My but that wine is strong . . . it makes one teeter . . . like a king on his throne . . .

DRUNKARD: Har, har, har! As a matter of fact, it seems it would suffice to touch glasses!

DIGNITARY/TRAITOR: To touch glasses in the presence of the entire Court!

DRUNKARD: Then, if someone touched the King . . .

DIGNITARY/TRAITOR: Quite unexpectedly!

DRUNKARD: Touched . . .

DIGNITARY/TRAITOR: Just like that, in front of everybody! For all to see!

DRUNKARD: Har, har, har! But nobody's going to touch the King because everyone is afraid of the Prince's anger and wisdom. It's only natural for a son to defend his father . . .

DIGNITARY/TRAITOR: Another glass! But what if the Prince himself . . . if the Prince himself went up to him and . . . I didn't really mean that, though you must admit it's a tempting idea. . . . I confess that whenever I see such an untouchable person . . . damn it, I don't know why, I always get the urge . . . to go up and . . . er . . . well . . . touch him, see? With my finger. Hm, hm . . .

DRUNKARD: Har, har, har, har, har! And there's his fiancée standing in back of him and, damn it, she's untouchable too. . . . Untouchable! Oh, if I could just touch him with one finger at least, with just one little finger, oh, oh, oh, and har, har, har!

Act II

HENRY:

Finger!

(*Calmly.*) There's that idiotic finger again!

You pig!

DRUNKARD (*gloomily*):

You pig!

HENRY:

You pig!

May I offer you some pastry?

COURT:

How pleasant it is at His Majesty's tea

To carry on a flirt in a form so discreet . . .

HENRY:

And you would like me

To touch the King . . . with my finger . . . Because if
   I touch the King

Then you'll touch him too, right? . . . You'd have me

Commit treason . . . is that it?

BOTH:

Oh, oh!

That was just the wine in us speaking . . . A drop
   of that stuff

And a man's liable to say anything!

HENRY: You goddamn drunken swine, you're trying to get me drunk. . . . Well, in a second I'll prove to you and to myself how sober I am . . . that's right, sober.

This intrigue is absurd. But this absurdity is likewise deceiving. Because this intrigue is so irrational, so obviously contrived that even if I rejected your rather naïve propositions, in the end I would come out looking just as ridiculous as if I'd agreed to them. That's what you had in mind all along, isn't it? And so I hereby declare both to you and to myself that I regard none of this seriously—neither you, nor this conversation, nor the title of this man who only a short while ago was nothing but an ordinary drunkard. I don't give a damn about the lot of you! And if I stand here talking to you instead of pouncing on you and touching you—it's only because I wish to keep up appearances and, if possible, avoid a scandal. . . . So there! Am I sober or not?

DRUNKARD:

A glass of Burgundy or a glass of Tokay!

DIGNITARY/TRAITOR:

A glass of Tokay or a glass of port!

HENRY: Of course I'm sober! I could wake up at any moment and annihilate you all—but I don't wish to spoil this magnificent and intoxicating reception . . . and besides, then my fiancée would disappear too, evaporate. . . . Understand?

DRUNKARD:

Burgundy, Burgundy!

DIGNITARY/TRAITOR:

Tokay, Tokay!

HENRY: I am the most sober person in the world! I am behaving in the same manner as you are, but with full awareness, soberly, har, har, har. . . . I am behaving in the same manner as you are, because to tell the truth, all of this gives me pleasure . . .

> Words tickle me, thoughts caress me, the passions get stronger
> Everything is spinning . . . singing . . . ringing
> Oh, this sea of lights, this ocean of words
> And I'm drowning in it, drowning, drowning . . . like a drunkard
> (See how sober I am!?)

I'm unsteady on my feet and I'm seeing three of
everything
I'm hearing things and my vision's getting blurry
It's almost as though I understood, but I don't under-
stand . . .
Noise. Noise. And in this noise
One thought alone persists: keep up appearances

Don't let anyone catch on you're drunk, har, har (See
how lucid I am!?) and don't let anyone know you're
a drunkard.
And so, if anyone addresses me in a polite tone, I'll
answer him with extreme politeness, ah, ah, yes, yes!
And if anyone begins speaking to me in a serious tone,
I'll answer him in a serious tone, ho, ho, yes indeed, yes
indeed!
And if anyone starts behaving toward me like a drunkard, I'll behave toward him like a drunkard too, hee,
hee, hic, hic! (You can see for yourselves how lucid I
am . . .)

DRUNKARD (*drunk*):
Son-of-a . . . Oh, f-f-f-fiddlesticks!
Shit!

HENRY:
Wait a minute, wait a minute
I'll show you even more clearly how sober I am. Let's
assume
You are soused too—and that everyone here
Is a little . . . hmm . . . One person gets drunk by
means of another
While each would pretend he's as sober as I. Har,
har, har!
But if that were the case, then this is all a farce!

One drunkard, in order to pretend he's sober, adapts
himself to the drunkenness of another who, in order to

pretend he's sober, adapts himself to the drunkenness of
still another drunkard who . . .

> And consequently all of this is just a lie! Nobody says
> What he wants to say, only what's considered proper.
>   Words
> Join together behind our backs like traitors
> And it is not we who say words, but words which say
>   us
> And betray our thoughts, which in turn betray
> Our treasonous feelings . . . Oh, treason!
> (*Drunk.*) Incessant treason!

DRUNKARD (*picking up the thread*): That's right, treason!

DIGNITARY/TRAITOR:
> Treason! Down with the King!
> Down with the King!

TRAITORS (*gathering around them, in an undertone*):
> Down with the King!

HENRY: Traitors! That's not what I wanted to say!

DIGNITARY/TRAITOR (*in the voice of a conspirator*):
> Gentlemen, the Prince is with us! Down with the King!
> Long live the new King!

TRAITORS: Long live the new King!

DRUNKARD: Down with the King!

> HENRY *and the* CONSPIRATORS *advance toward the* KING.
> *The* GUESTS *make way, revealing the* KING, *who is taking
> his tea in the company of the* QUEEN *and* MOLLY. JOHNNY
> *is standing nearby.*

HENRY: That's not what I wanted to say!

COURT:
> *How pleasant it is at His Majesty's tea*

To carry on a flirt in a form so discreet
Oh, the toupees and décolletés do the senses arouse
While His Majesty himself does the honors of the
house!

FATHER (*uneasy, seeing the* DRUNKARD *approach*): Now what does he want?

HENRY: This gentleman is a foreign envoy or else an ambassador!

FATHER: An ambassador, eh? Whatever you do, don't make a fool of yourself. . . . (*Aloud.*) It is indeed a pleasure, Your Excellency, to welcome you under our roof.

DRUNKARD: I am both honored and flattered, Your Majesty. (*He bows down before* MOLLY.) Permit me, O loveliest of maidens, to adorn the bosom of your best man with the flower of my chivalrous homage.

MOLLY: Thank you.

FATHER: It is my sincerest wish, Mr. Ambassador, that relations between our two powerful governments in accord with international harmony and co-operation and with a view to consolidating and safeguarding, as well as everlasting peace which for centuries has constituted the guiding principle, and in the interest of mankind. If ya touch me, ya pig, I'll clobber ya in the kisser and slap ya in irons.

DRUNKARD: The consolidation and safeguarding as well as mankind in the spirit of co-operation and in the interest of everlasting peace constitutes the guiding and inviolable principle of our peaceful aspirations that are enlivened by the spirit of mutual understanding. I'm gonna touch ya, see . . . I'm gonna blow myself up, you pig, and lay ya out flat . . .

FATHER: May I offer you some pastry?

DRUNKARD: That's terribly kind of you. (*To* HENRY, *aside.*)
Quick! Now's the time! Stick your finger in his belly!

HENRY: My father?

DRUNKARD: Then afterwards *you* will be King!

HENRY (*musingly*): Me?

The stage becomes motionless.

I'm only joking, of course . . . But what if . . . To overthrow this father and seize power! To be in control of
the situation! To be in control!

Everything keeps slipping away from me! It's terrible! I
am no longer master of the situation! I'm like a puppet
in a puppet show. To control! Oh, if only I had control!
To govern!

No, no, I was only joking, of course. . . . But what if I
were to overthrow this King! What do I need him for
anyway? I made him King so he could grant me a marriage. But why should I let myself be married by someone else? If I were to become master, I could grant myself
a marriage—and a decent and respectable one too. Then
I would be the one who makes laws. I would be the one
who decides what is holy, what is virtuous, what is a
sacrament—I would be the one who decides everything!

Oh, God! If only I could be in control!

Oh, God! What God? Oh, Father! What father? It was
I who made them what they are. By virtue of my bounty!
By virtue of my will! Why should I kneel down before
them? Why not kneel down before myself, myself, myself,
the sole source of my law?

Shhh! . . . Don't say that. Why do you say that? You're
only repeating what he (*points to the* DRUNKARD) said.

Well so what if he said it? I'll destroy him too!
It is I who create kings!
It is I who should be King!

I am supreme! There is nothing higher than me!
I am God!

And it is my finger, my finger, which . . . (*Frightened.*)
No, it isn't true! I didn't mean it! It isn't true! I wouldn't
betray my father for anything in the world! My King!

(*To the* DRUNKARD.) I shall not betray him!

DRUNKARD: You won't betray him, you pig?

FATHER (*who has been listening*): What, what, what? . . .
Treason? . . .

HENRY: That's not what I wanted to say!

FATHER: Don't you come near me!

HENRY: I'm not coming near you.

FATHER: Don't move! Don't anybody move!

HENRY: I'm not moving. (*Despairingly.*) Why are you afraid
of me?

FATHER: Me? Henry, my son, my child, how could I be afraid
of you, my friend, my defender, my support? No, no,
Henry, I'm not afraid . . .

HENRY: Calm yourself . . .

FATHER:
Adjust my sash, oh, oh,
Adjust my sash . . .

HENRY (*adjusting the sash*):
He's trembling, his heart is pounding and his cheeks
Are bathed with sweat . . .

FATHER (*quietly*): Tssst . . . Henry . . .

HENRY: What is it?

FATHER: You'd better go away. . . . Go away.

The Marriage

HENRY: Why?

FATHER: Henry, why should I be afraid of you? . . . Oh, perhaps just a little bit, just a tiny bit, maybe just a teeny-weeny bit—you know, just in case. . . . But I am the King, Henry, so I think you'd better leave me now, because even though it's small, being royal it might grow . . . it might become gigantic . . . and then one day it might explode! And the King and me might get carried away!

HENRY: Calm down . . . Control yourself . . .

FATHER: How can I control myself if I am . . . greater than myself?

HENRY: Shhh! . . . Don't shout!

FATHER:

I'm not shouting

It's my voice which is shouting! Tssst . . . (*In a loud voice.*) Thank you, my son, for your loyalty! I know in your filial heart there isn't any treason. No, there isn't any! I haven't the slightest bit of doubt. Not the slightest . . . and if I say I haven't any doubts, it's not because

I have any; and if I emphasize
That I say it not because of that, it's just
So nobody will think I'm coming back to it

For some other reason. But what I just got through explaining should likewise not be interpreted as a sign of

My distrust. (*To the* DIGNITARIES.) Stop
Listening to me! Why
Do you listen to me all the time? Why

Don't you stop gawking at me? Do you think it's very pleasant to be listened to and gawked at all the time? Get out of here, out, out!

98

No, no, stay here! I
Have nothing to hide. If I tell you
To get out, it does not mean at all

that I have something to hide. No, no, I don't have any
doubts as far as my son is concerned; I am positive he is
not a traitor, I have no doubts whatsoever, none whatsoever. . . . For if I had even the slightest bit of doubt
in this respect, even so much as the slightest, then this
tiny grain of doubt would, in the presence of so many,
many people and the expectation of so many, many
people . . . this doubt, I say, this tiny, insignificant
doubt . . . would become larger . . . just a tiny bit larger
. . . and that larger doubt would provoke a light trembling which, being a royal trembling, would provoke a
great panic . . . and then an even greater one . . . greater
than me even . . . and that panic would carry me away,
because the King is carrying me away! ! And if the King
trembles, I cannot stop him from trembling! And if the
King shouts, I cannot make him lower his voice! And
the King, the King, the King is shouting: treason! Treason! Treason!

COURT: Treason!

HENRY: Treason!

FATHER:
Help! Guards! Guards!

The GUARDS *rush in.*

He has a finger!
Oh, treason, treason, treason!

HENRY (*touching the* FATHER *with his finger*):
Arrest
Arrest this father of mine! And cast him
Into some dark and dreary,
Foul and oppressive

99

Godforsaken dungeon!
(*Despairingly.*) That's not what I wanted to say!

DRUNKARD (*with delight*): He toushhed him! He toushhed
him in the belly! (*He makes a gesture as though he is
going to attack the* FATHER.)

HENRY (*to* JOHNNY, *indicating the* DRUNKARD):
Arrest
This pig! And into the dungeon with him!
(*To everyone.*) I don't know how it happened
But it happened! I betrayed
My father!
(*To the* DRUNKARD.) What time is it?

DRUNKARD: Seven.

FATHER (*groaning*):
Henreee . . .

COURT (*thunderously*):
Oh, Henry!

HENRY (*thunderously*):
Oh, Henry!
Now *I* am King!
Bind him, break his bones and trample him under-
foot!

The GUARDS *arrest the* FATHER.

MOTHER (*in a shrill voice*): Henry, dear, what are you doing?

HENRY:
Now I shall rule! I alone!

I shall get married on my own! And nobody is going to
stand in my way! I've just had the old man placed under
arrest. That drunkard has likewise been taken into custody. Now I am King, now I am the one who is in control,
now I shall get married on my own . . .

100

Enough of this idle chatter! Do you think
That I am blind? That I don't see

How you're trying to make a chump out of me? But
that's all over now. I'm not going to dance to your tune
any more. I'm not going to be your puppet on a string.
I'll force you to obey and respect my will. If the old
man's afraid to rule, if he's unable to marry me, I'll get
married by myself. Where is my fiancée? (*Seeing* MOLLY
approach.)

Ah, here she comes. She has ceased to be pure
But don't worry, I shall purify her! I shall lead her
out of here!
I shall grant myself a marriage! I alone!
Let nobody try to interfere! I shall do it myself!
Because I am alone here, I am alone here
And none of you are here!

Procession. HENRY *and* MOLLY *lead. Wedding march.*

I am marching at the head . . . What do I care
If the others are trailing behind me like a tail
I cannot see them. I am passing
Through pure space, an empty void . . .

(*Noticing the* DRUNKARD *who is being guarded by* JOHNNY.)
And get that imbecile out of here, eliminate him. . . . Do
away with him. . . . You won't get off very easily with
me. . . . Sentence him to death!

DRUNKARD (*in the voice of a beggar*): Master . . . Master . . .

HENRY: That sounded pretty silly, didn't it? . . . Well, you
won't be doing me any more harm where you're going!

DRUNKARD: Your Majesty! Ah, what's the use! So much the
worse for me! Very well. So be it then! (*To everyone.*)
They're going to hang me, they're going to hang me!

101

That's all they've been doing around here for the last few years—hanging people! (*To* HENRY.) Sire, I have but one request to make before I die. That I might be permitted to have one last look at her.

HENRY: Who?

DRUNKARD: My Queen.

HENRY: I bet he's up to another one of his tricks. But I am not afraid any more—everything is dependent on my will now.

> All right, go ahead.
> You're looking at her.

DRUNKARD (*to himself*): Oh, Molly, Molly—would I like to have a snort of you!

HENRY (*to himself*): Har, har, har!

DRUNKARD: I didn't marry you, and now it's someone else's turn.

HENRY: Let him say whatever he pleases. (*To* JOHNNY.) Keep a close watch on him.

DRUNKARD: If I didn't have this joker on my back, if I hadn't been arrested—I'd've known how to . . . with you, me, me and you . . .

HENRY: He's talking gibberish.

DRUNKARD: I shall carry the image of your angelic face with me always unto the four walls of my coffin, and there with your image before me I shall turn up my toes . . . hic . . . (*To* HENRY.) Sire, I beseech you to grant me this one last favor—ask this young fella here (*points to* JOHNNY) to take a flower out of that vase and hold it a li'l bit

102

above Her Majesty's precious li'l head while I stand over here and watch.

HENRY: This is another of his idiotic pranks, but if I refuse everyone will get the idea I'm afraid . . . so I'd better not refuse. (*To* JOHNNY.) Do as he says. (*To* MOLLY.) My dearest Mary, I trust you will see it in your heart to grant this pathetic maniac his last dying wish.

DRUNKARD: Oh, my Queen! My only wish is to die with your image before my eyes. . . . I humbly entreat you to hold the flower jus' a li'l bit lower . . . so it barely comes down over her eyes . . . (*While lowering the flower,* JOHNNY *embraces* MARY.) Now jus' a li'l bit lower . . . that's it, that's it . . . Oh, my Queen!

HENRY: What's he trying to prove? It doesn't mean a thing.

DIGNITARIES (*waking up, theatrically*):
      It doesn't mean a thing
      It's quite harmless!
      Poor soul!
      It's rather amusing.

DRUNKARD: Excuse me, jus' a li'l bit lower . . . so the flower barely touches her neck. . . . Oh, that's it, that's it, perfect. . . . Oh, how ravishing . . .

DIGNITARIES:
      One must admire the patience of His Majesty.
      Not only is he just but he's generous too.
      One must admire the patience of Her Majesty
      Her Majesty is exceedingly generous!

DRUNKARD (*unexpectedly, gravely*): And now don't either of you move, 'cuz I'm gonna take away the flower. (*He pulls the flower out of* JOHNNY's *hand.*) Don't move . . .

MOLLY: This is just like posing for a photograph.

HENRY (*to* JOHNNY *and* MOLLY): Wait a second. (*To himself.*) Well, so what? (*To* JOHNNY.) Don't move. (*To himself.*) I wonder what he's up to?

This is absurd. I thought he was more clever . . .

DRUNKARD: Clever.

HENRY: Clever?

DRUNKARD: Clever . . .

HENRY: What do you mean, clever? What's so clever about that? The flower's already been discarded and they're still standing in the same artificial position . . . Clever?

DRUNKARD: Clever . . .

HENRY: Clever?
    What of it? They're standing there together . . . So?
        They're standing together . . .
    Ah, the two of them together . . . He with her, and she
    With him . . . Well, so what if they are? Together
    But it doesn't make any sense . . . They're standing
        there in an artificial manner. Wait a minute . . .
    Well, what of it? . . . They're standing there, and the
        rest of us
    Are looking on . . . While they go on standing there . . .
    You pig!
    You've bound them together
    By a dreadful
    And inferior bond. You've married them
    You pig priest!

DRUNKARD: You pig!

HENRY: You pig!

    Laughter of the DIGNITARIES.

ACT III

A hall in the castle; HENRY *and the* CHANCELLOR.

CHANCELLOR: There is peace. All the rebellious elements are under arrest. Congress has also been taken into custody along with military and civilian circles, vast segments of the population, the Supreme Court, the Joint Chiefs of Staff, Boards and Departments, all public and private authorities, the press, hospitals and orphanages. All the Ministries have been placed under arrest, and everything else besides; in short, Your Majesty—everything. The police have likewise been imprisoned. There is peace. Quiet. It's humid.

HENRY: Indeed. There is peace. How calm it is.

CHANCELLOR: Well, what did you expect? It's autumn.

HENRY: Where is the Chief of Police?

CHANCELLOR: He's waiting.

HENRY: Well, as long as he's waiting, let him wait. And what about my father, the ex-King?

CHANCELLOR: Under arrest.

HENRY: And that . . . drunkard?

CHANCELLOR: Under arrest.

HENRY (*gloomily, bitterly*): Today's the wedding. . . . What a miserable day!

CHANCELLOR: A day like any other.

105

HENRY: You're getting old.

CHANCELLOR: I'm afraid so.

HENRY:

I am in power.
Never mind how I came by it. I took control
Of the situation . . . and so everything will be
As I command . . . Therefore I command
Everyone to assemble here, in this hall, because the
King has decided
To bestow a marriage on himself.
Now take those louts by the snouts and drag them in
here!

CHANCELLOR: Yes, Your Majesty.

HENRY: Have my father brought in under heavy guard. By the snout. I wish to get married in his presence.

CHANCELLOR: Yes, Your Majesty.

HENRY: And have my mother brought in, too. By the snout.

CHANCELLOR: Yes, Your Majesty.

HENRY: And that drunkard too . . . but securely bound, mind you. I want everyone to be present when I administer the sacrament to myself. I'm not afraid of anybody. Nobody can do me any harm. I alone know what I must do, and that's that. I am in command now and so everything will be done according to my will. I am in control; I am in control of the situation. If anybody conspires against me or tries to commit acts of sabotage, take the lout by the snout and . . . Has the Chief of Police arrived with his henchmen? Show them in.

Enter the CHIEF OF POLICE *and three of his* HENCHMEN.

HENRY: Just what I needed! Look at these snouts! Ho, ho, these snouts will take them by the snouts! Yes siree! If

anybody gets out of line or in any way tries to interfere
or cause trouble, take the lout by the snout and slap him
silly in front of everybody . . . for all to see . . .

CHANCELLOR: I'm afraid, Sire, that . . . Let's see, what was it
I wanted to say?

HENRY: My head is clear. Listen to my way of reasoning.
Please, listen to my way of reasoning. I have already lost
my innocence. They robbed me of my virginity. Lately,
though, I've been doing a lot of thinking on my own. I
didn't sleep a wink last night!

Holiness, majesty, power, law, morality, love, ridiculousness, stupidity, wisdom—all these come from people
in the same way that wine comes from grapes. Like wine,
understand? I have the situation well in hand and I shall
force these apes to produce everything my heart desires.
And if that is ridiculous, I'll take that ridiculousness
by the snout too! And if that is foolish, I'll take that
foolishness by the snout too! And if God, old antediluvian
God, has anything against it, I'll take him by the snout
too! . . .

CHANCELLOR *and* CHIEF: Yes, Your Majesty!

HENCHMEN: Yes, Your Majesty!

HENRY: Yes, Your Majesty!

ALL: Yes, Your Majesty!

Enter PANDULF.

PANDULF: No!

HENRY: No?

PANDULF: No!

HENRY: Well, I'll be d . . . If it isn't the Bishop!

PANDULF:

I am Pandulf.

A cardinal of the Roman Catholic Church, and I
    declare this

To your face, you infamous usurper: God exists

And a marriage not consecrated by the Church

Is not a marriage, but a sacrilege!

HENRY:

Har, har, har, Pandulf, Pandulf!

(*Derisively.*) My dear Pandulf,

You are Pandulf, are you not?

PANDULF:

Yes, I am Pandulf.

HENRY:

Ah . . . and you're

A cardinal too, if I'm not mistaken? . . .

PANDULF:

I am a servant of God

A servant of God, I, Pandulf . . .

HENRY:

My dear Pandulf, you aren't by any chance . . . a little
    tipsy

Tipsy

Tipsy

With this Pandulf of yours? Well? My dear Pandulf,
    you aren't a little bit tight

Tight

Tight

With this cardinal of yours? The cardinal has gone to
    your head. Booze

Booze

Booze

108

But, my dear Pandulf, you are absolutely blind drunk with your Lord God and the Holy Catholic Church. You're nothing but an ordinary drunkard, Pandulf. Shame on you! Oh, I know all about it. First one glass, then another, pretty soon—away you go! No, Pandulf, you're no ordinary fellow. You're a drunkard!

PANDULF:
> I curse
> You!

HENRY: What? Are you nipping again? Are you getting pickled on your own curse in my presence? Well, this has gone far enough. I'm going to touch you. (*He touches him.*)

PANDULF: Oh, God . . .

HENRY:
> Arrest this rummy priest!
> Arrest him. Come on, henchmen,
> Take him by the snout!

> PANDULF *is whisked offstage by the* HENCHMEN.

What a miserable day!

CHANCELLOR: Yes, it's a miserable day . . .

HENRY: I am ruling . . .

CHANCELLOR: Yes, Your Majesty.

HENRY: I shall rule . . .

CHANCELLOR: Yes, Your Majesty.

HENRY: I'm going to touch everybody.

CHANCELLOR: Yes, Your Majesty.

HENRY:
> No one will dare to touch me . . . By the way,
> My dear Chancellor,

Tell me, people aren't by any chance making fun of me
    a little
Are they? . . .

CHANCELLOR: Oh, oh, oh!

CHIEF: Oh, oh, oh!

HENRY:
They aren't saying
Behind my back somewhere, and
Behind their own backs too, that . . . that . . . that . . .
That I'm jealous, for example, har, har! Well, are
    they? That would be
A laugh, wouldn't it?

CHANCELLOR: Oh, oh, oh!

CHIEF: Oh, oh, oh!

HENRY:
I only ask
On account of that silly little episode
With the flower, har, har har! The insinuation
Made by that contemptible drunkard left little room
    for doubt
And may have given more fodder
To these foul and slippery tongues, har, har, har!

CHANCELLOR: I know nothing about it!

CHIEF: We know nothing about it!

HENRY:
Because
If he connected them in such a singular position
Then they are connected . . . and perhaps others
Are likewise connecting them . . . her with him, and
    him
With her . . . Well? Speak up! Perhaps

No one will have the nerve to say it openly
But that won't stop them from smirking, insinuating,
    or winking with one eye,
Exchanging meaningful glances or signaling on the
    sly, har, har, har . . .

My throat is dry. My throat has gone dry. Hey, servant,
bring me an apple! I'm going to have an apple! (*To the*
CHANCELLOR.) Well? Well?

CHANCELLOR: Properly speaking, Your Majesty, everyone is
acting properly, but then again, properly speaking, perhaps improperly too, who knows; perhaps people are
insinuating things, and then again, maybe they aren't,
how should I know, I'm nearsighted, my vision isn't what
it used to be . . .

HENRY: You blind old nag! You blind old gopher!

CHIEF: I'm nearsighted too.

HENRY: I'll let the air out of both of you . . . (*To the* SERVANT
who has brought the apple.) Wait a moment. Stand still,
let me get a good look at you. Who knows what this man
might be

    Thinking

In private, up there. . . . Look at him! He's a numskull,
one of those shady types. But who knows? Perhaps

    He's imagining something. Perhaps in his mind
    He's connecting . . .
    He's connecting the two of them there . . .
    Perhaps he's making fun of me in private
    And betraying me . . . with him . . . and with her . . .
    Oh, the traitors!

They're betraying me! They're nothing but a bunch of
traitors! And this immobile face. How do I know but

at this very moment he isn't laughing at me or insinuating something awful, whether inwardly he isn't howling with laughter. . . . This apple is lying *between* my knife and fork. Knife and fork. What's it doing *between* my knife and fork? Oh, yes, of course, that's how they always serve apples, peaches, pears. . . . No, besides it's absurd. There was never anything between Johnny and her. . . . No, it's just my imagination. . . . I know it's idiotic and yet
      I have to say it . . . and saying it
      I declare it . . .

CHANCELLOR (*to the* CHIEF):
                              His Majesty
      Is curiously absorbed with his thoughts . . .
CHIEF:
                              He's probably
      Troubled by unwholesome dreams.

HENRY (*to himself*):
      I don't want to drink any more
      I'm not going to drink any more . . .

CHANCELLOR (*aside*):
      Tch, tch, tch, vodka, vodka!

HENRY (*to himself*):
      Until now perhaps
      There has never been anything between them, but now
      That everybody connects them, maybe he connects him-
            self
      With her too . . . And connecting himself with her
      Touches her . . .

CHANCELLOR:
      Oh, oh, oh, vodka, vodka . . .

HENRY (*to himself*):
      I hear what I'm saying

And I hear what he's saying. And I know perfectly well
That what we're both saying is pure comedy
All the same, I must speak . . .

CHANCELLOR (*delightedly, aloud*):
   The king is gassed!

HENRY (*to the* CHANCELLOR): Shut your trap! (*He slaps the*
CHIEF OF POLICE *in the face.*)

CHIEF: Why me?

HENRY:
   Just to keep you guessing! At the moment
   I am in need of a little brutality—and I'm searching
      for it

In your face! If I'd struck the Chancellor, I would have
been acting only justly. But I want to be brutal! I'm
going to establish order here! (*Cries are heard.*) Now
what's the matter?

MOTHER (*offstage*):
   Let go of me, let go!
   (*She bursts in.*)
   Oh, Henry, my little Henry, your father, your father,
      your father!

HENRY: Has she gone mad?

MOTHER:
   Oh, Henry, your father's yelling, your father's scream-
      ing
   Ranting and raving like an animal, jumping up
   And down!

HENRY: He must have gone crazy!

MOTHER (*dramatically, lyrically*):
   He tried to break loose, he tried to escape

> Far, far away, into the hills
> But they caught 'im
> And now they're whippin' his ass
> Oh, Henry, he's a pain in your ass!

HENRY: So? What's that got to do with me?

MOTHER:
> Oh, a knife, a knife, a knife!

HENRY: I hold my knife this way.

MOTHER (*terrified*):
> For God's sake, Henry!
> I'm your mother!

HENRY: That's right—you are my mother. What a happy coincidence . . . (*He walks up to her.*) I'd like to hug you and kiss you, mamma . . . (*He puts his arms around her.*)

MOTHER: Henry, what are you doing?

HENRY: I'm hugging you.

MOTHER:
> You'd better leave me alone
> There's something odd about the way you hug me
> No, no, leave me in peace!

CHANCELLOR: That's odd, that's odd . . .

CHIEF: Odd, positively distasteful . . .

> FATHER *bursts in, followed by the* HENCHMEN.

FATHER: Help! They're beating me!

MOTHER: Murderers!

FATHER (*quietly*):
> They beat me

(*Louder.*) They beat me
(*Shouting.*) They beat me! Me! Me!

MOTHER: Come here, he beat me too.

FATHER (*shouting*): What? What? Has he been beating you?

MOTHER: Quiet, quiet, shh . . .

FATHER (*in a lower voice*): Just for that I'll curse the son-of-
a . . .

MOTHER: Shh! Shh!

FATHER: What? What was that you said? He hit you?

HENRY: Lucky thing I have this knife . . .

ALL: Oh!

HENRY:

No, what an idea! I'm not going to kill anyone, even
though this knife
Is sharpening me!
I'm not going to kill anyone—I'm merely going
To touch them . . .
(*He touches his* MOTHER *and* FATHER.)
O cruel and abominable couple
Who would their own son curse! Father and mother!
Holy of holies! But
I am touching them
Look how I'm touching them, look how I'm moving
them, look how I'm digging into their gut!

CHANCELLOR:

Never before
Have my poor old eyes
Seen such a sight . . .

CHIEF:

Never in a million years
Would I have imagined anything like this!

The Marriage

A HENCHMAN: What a disgrace!

FATHER: May you croak!

MOTHER: Would that your mother had suffered a miscarriage!

FATHER: May your father strangle you to death!

MOTHER: May you never have any children!

FATHER: May your children turn you out in your old age!

MOTHER: May they strangle you to death!

FATHER: May they pluck out your eyes!

HENRY:
Take them way!
They're drunk, drunk on motherhood and fatherhood!
But I am sober!

The HENCHMEN *converge upon the* MOTHER *and* FATHER.

FATHER:
Henreee . . .

HENRY: What is it?

FATHER:
Henr-e-e-e

Henr-e-e-e, Henr-e-e-e, I realize you've taken the King
away from me . . . but I'm still your father after all. . . .
For God's sake, Henry, don't deprive me of the father,
because if you do, the universe will burst into smithereens
with such an earsplitting, god-awful racket . . .

HENRY: Father is a title the same as King is. Can't you speak
like an ordinary man? Must you always get dressed up in
some title or other?

I feel sleepy. Take them away!

Act III

FATHER:

> With these words
> You open the gates to a terrible misfortune
> Oh, Lord

MOTHER: Have mercy . . .

CHANCELLOR: On us sinners . . . (*He pulls a newspaper out of his pocket.*) War has been declared!

HENRY: What? What war?

CHANCELLOR:

> I received this newspaper
> Only a moment ago.

Silence. In the distance, sounds of a cannon exploding.

HENRY: It's true—they're shooting.

FATHER: It sounds like it's coming from the forest . . .

General anxiety.

MOTHER: We'd better start packing.

CHANCELLOR: If necessary we can go down into the basement.

FATHER: Artillery is nothing. The worst is poison gas. We'd better stock up on supplies. . . . (*To* MOTHER.) Go out and buy whatever you can—the stores will be closed soon.

MOTHER: I've got some gas masks around here somewhere . . . but where? I've got them somewhere, but I can't remember . . . which drawer it was . . . (*With growing uneasiness.*) Where have I been keeping them?

An explosion.

CHIEF: It's getting closer.

CHANCELLOR:

> Sire, will you give
> The orders?

117

HENRY: I'm not giving any orders, because none of this is real!
It isn't real! But it *is* real!
(*Straining his ear.*)
Oh, listen to them fight!

FATHER: What'll become of us? What'll become of us now?
Oh, misfortune, conflagration, rape, torture, infamy, dishonor . . .

HENRY:
That's a lot of rubbish! Just some sort
Of drunken ravings! They're both reeking
With liquor! Throw them out!

FATHER (*drunk*):
Hic! . . . I'm drunk . . . Hic! . . So be it then
My son has said so . . . Well, such is life . . .
But seein' as I'm already a little tight, then before you
stick me in the
Dungeon, what d'ya say me and you have a little
Snort, eh? I'm gonna let ya in on a li'l secret! I'm
gonna whishper something in your ear
That'll go straight to your head . . .

MOTHER (*drunk*): Tra-la-la . . .

FATHER:
Don't marry that girl!
That old drunk was telling you the truth. She
Used to whore around with your friend Johnny.

HENRY: That's a lie!

FATHER:
I'm telling you the truth!

I didn't want to tell you before because I was too
ashamed, but seein' as everything has gone to hell anyway . . .

On the very same day
You and she got engaged, I
Caught 'em in the bushes, stumbled across 'em there in
the bushes,
And stepped on 'em with my foot!

HENRY:

It isn't true!
And yet it *is* true!

MOTHER:

I caught 'em too once
Snuggled up together by the well
They were playin' footsie with each other
Right there in broad daylight! Don't marry that girl,
Henry!

Sound of an explosion.

HENRY: They've started up again!

FATHER (*looking out the window*): Soldiers.

CHANCELLOR: Soldiers.

MOTHER: They're just kids. Greenhorns.

FATHER: Maybe so, but they're already bleeding.

MOTHER:

Henry, don't you marry that girl!
She used to smile at the younger ones too
She used to fool around with the younger ones too!

FATHER:

She bled a lot
With men younger than she!

MOTHER:

In the bushes
Under some tree, or in the hay . . .

FATHER: In the cellar!

MOTHER: Or in the attic!

FATHER: In the barn!

MOTHER: Or in the coach house!

FATHER:
> In her panties
> Or without her panties!
> (*Gazing out the window.*) Ohh,
> look how they're strangling that guy,
> Look how they're mashing him . . . Now
> They're sticking him with a bayonet!

MOTHER: O ruin and conflagration!

FATHER: We'd better cover the window with something—if they spot us, they might come in here after us.

HENRY:
> You degenerate old
> Flea-bitten boozer,
> And you, you rickety, old,
> Whiskey-guzzling floozy . . . I've been far too
> Lenient
> And far too patient
> With your rotgut ravings! But now
> You will know my wrath! Out! Out! Out! I am alone!
> Lock them in irons!

The MOTHER *and* FATHER *are taken way by the* HENCHMEN.

FATHER: Have mercy on us!

HENRY: I shall grant this marriage myself! I shall marry her, I'll get married on my own! The rest is nothing but the foulmouthed ravings of some drunken fools! Blah-blah, blah! Bring my fiancée in here at once! It's time we began discussing the details of our nuptial ceremony. But first . . .

CHANCELLOR: But first . . .

HENRY: But first . . .

CHANCELLOR: But first . . .

HENRY: But first . . .
Summon my courtier this . . . what's his name . . . John
. . . that's it . . . John, my courtier . . . I must have a few
words with him . . . and with her . . .

All exeunt.

. . . and now we'll find out if there's anything between
them . . . and if there is . . .

Enter JOHNNY.

. . . we'll settle the matter once and for all. (*To* JOHNNY.)
Oh, it's you, Johnny. How are you getting along?

JOHNNY: Not bad.

HENRY: Not bad, not bad and not bad with me either! Johnny,
I'm afraid we've become involved in some . . . not
altogether pleasant affair . . .

JOHNNY: I don't care. It's better than being in the army.

HENRY: What time is it?

JOHNNY: Five-thirty.

HENRY: Where did you get that watch?

JOHNNY: I bought it in Antwerp.

HENRY: What's going on there? I understand war has been
declared.

JOHNNY: So I've heard.

HENRY: But you don't know for certain.

JOHNNY: Can anything be known for certain? You know, Henry, if I were you I wouldn't believe a word anyone says around here. . . . There's something false and pretentious about everything here . . .

HENRY: You're right, Johnny, nothing is real around here. . . . Everyone pretends to be himself and lies in order to tell the truth. . . . It's even a little amusing, if you ask me. . . . But I've already gotten used to it. And what about yourself, Johnny . . . are you a little . . . hm . . . tight too?

JOHNNY: Me?

HENRY: Everyone around here is getting drunk on something different. And so I thought perhaps you'd been . . . drinking something too.

JOHNNY: No.

HENRY: Well, then why do you look so sad?

JOHNNY: Me? I'm not sad at all. Quite the contrary.

HENRY (*sadly*): In appearance you aren't, but all the same you are . . . and your sadness is lurking in the shadows. . . . Hallo, hallo, come on out here, come on out here!

MOLLY *emerges from the shadows.*

What's new?

MOLLY: Nothing.

HENRY: How have you been?

MOLLY: All right.

HENRY: I have something to tell you . . . both of you. . . . You won't believe it but ever since that drunkard joined you together with the flower, har, har, har, in such a peculiar

position, into a statue, har, har, har, I can't get rid of
the impression that there's something between you two
. . . that something's going on between you two . . . har,
har, har!

> Har, har, har!
> Har, har, har!
> Well, how do I know!

JOHNNY: What's that supposed to mean? That you're jealous?

HENRY: You're speaking to me, but for *whom* are you speaking?

JOHNNY: I don't understand.

HENRY: You're standing there as if you were alone—but with
whom are you standing? (*To* MOLLY.) Why don't you
look at him?

MOLLY: Why should I?

HENRY: Even if you don't look at him, it's *him* you're not
looking at.

MOLLY (*theatrically*): Henry, I love you!

HENRY: Yes, you love me, and he is my friend. You love me
and you're a respectable girl . . . but what have you been
serving? (*To* JOHNNY.) And what have you been serving?

JOHNNY: What do you mean?

HENRY: Haven't you been serving evil? You have more crimes
on your conscience than a common criminal. You are
both respectable people, you are both innocent, you both
come from a good home . . . but what have you been
serving? So now

> You serve her, and let
> Her serve you!

123

MOLLY (*theatrically*): **Oh, don't torture me like this!**

HENRY: Both you and he love me . . . but only when *each of you is alone!* But the two of you . . . but the two of you *together* . . . Together you are altogether different from what you are separately!

JOHNNY: The two of us together are nothing, so stop persecuting us as well as yourself!

HENRY: Us! Us! Why do you say "us"? Ah, what strange things go on in this world of ours!

Imagine—after he threw away that flower, it suddenly became apparent that you were together . . . you must have been aware of that yourselves. . . . And now everyone is joining you together, and I am likewise joining you together . . . in my mind, of course . . . and you are becoming more and more intimately connected!

Oh, in some strange, inexplicable way that man has joined you together in wedlock! He must be a priest! An unholy priest of some mysterious rite. . . . A psychological priest!

JOHNNY: What's happening to you? You're all excited.

HENRY: Am I? I'm beginning to doubt whether I exist at all. It seems to me that I feel, that I think, that I make decisions . . . but in reality nothing is decided inside me; everything is decided between . . . between ourselves. . . . It's between ourselves that spring the forces, the charms, the gods, the illusions which toss us about like straws in the wind. . . . And we flounder along . . .

JOHNNY: How so?

HENRY: Look what happened to me, for instance. He joined you together in a certain way, stacked you one on top of the other, multiplied you one times the other—or again, he attached you to her and her to you—and made out of you something which excites me . . . which intoxicates me to such an extent that (*menacingly*) I shall not rest until I have married her. Remember that.

JOHNNY: I won't stand in your way.

HENRY: Oh, why has my nature brought me to this? Why after such a cloudy . . . cloudy . . . voyage have I put in to such a port? How is such a phenomenon to be explained? Perhaps secretly I harbor a certain affection for you—an inarticulate, illicit, amoral and abnormal affection.

JOHNNY: Whatever that's supposed to mean.

HENRY: Perhaps subconsciously I have been jealous about her all along . . . and of you . . . and regarded you all along as my rival?

JOHNNY: So what?

HENRY: All the same, who knows whether it is possible . . . whether in general it is possible for a man to fall in love with a woman without the co-operation, without the intermediary of another man? It may be that in general man is incapable of responding to a woman except through the intermediary of another man. Might this not be some new form of love? Before, only two were needed, but today it's three.

JOHNNY: I think you're exaggerating.

HENRY: Perhaps this is something which has been imposed on me from without; perhaps deep down inside I don't feel that way at all, but merely feel obliged to behave as though in fact I did. My head is spinning from this winding, tortuous road down which I keep walking, and walking . . . endlessly . . . without a moment's rest. . . . Oh, heavy are these gates, oppressive is this ceiling, strange and enigmatic is this sky.

Oh, that drunkard has made me drunk. Oh, that priest

125

really is a priest. With his finger . . . with his finger . . .
he has fashioned an idol out of you . . . before which I
must kneel and offer sacrifice as in a dream.

> The hell I will!
> I am still the King! It is I who rule!
> I shall rule! Oh, Henry, Henry, Henry! I am alone!
> I shall confer this marriage myself! Henry!
> Don't let yourself be ruled! You be the one who rules!
> Henry, cast down these gods, destroy these spells
> And your own throne ascend!

How strange that sounded. Damn it! If only I didn't have
to speak in such an artificial manner. And here she is . . .
standing right beside us . . . and listening.

MOLLY (*theatrically*): Why do you torture yourself and me so!

HENRY: What an insufferable ham! There are times when I'd
like to . . . (*Makes a gesture as though he is about to
strike her.*)

MOLLY (*in a vulgar tone*): Hey, don't pull any of that stuff
on me, buster!

HENRY:

> Leave me.
> I have to talk with him in private.
> Don't go too far away though. Have
> The servants bring you some tea.

MOLLY *goes out.*

> And now
> Let's get down to business. I only wish I knew the
>   outcome of all this.
> What a dreadful silence . . .
> These walls and everything around here is waiting pa-
>   tiently to hear
> What I am going to say.

It's been a long time since I've felt so jumpy. (*To* JOHNNY.) Ah, Johnny, how's it going?

JOHNNY: All right.

HENRY: I'd like to have a few words with you. Sit down.

JOHNNY: All right.

HENRY:
    I have something unpleasant to tell you
    Something which may even be a little abnormal
    In the sense that it's not altogether common or usual
    But departs rather from the normal course of events.

JOHNNY:
    What do I care if something's abnormal
    As long as I am normal!

HENRY:
    The point is if I told you in an ordinary manner
    It would not be convincing. Everything depends
    On how we speak. That is why
    I have to tell you this in a manner which is perhaps a
        trifle
    Artificial.

And I must ask you on your part not to respond to me in a normal manner, but to conduct yourself exactly as I tell you. No one will be coming in here. We'll lock the door.

JOHNNY: Do whatever you like.

HENRY: I know. You've already been forced to do so many strange things in spite of your youth. But I assure you this is not a caprice of mine, but something far more serious. As you know, my dear Johnny, I have deposed my father, the King, and ascended the throne myself.

And today I have decided to grant myself a marriage to my fiancée, Princess Mary. Say: Yes, I know.

JOHNNY: Yes, I know.

HENRY: But what's the sense of marrying her, even in the most formal manner, if the whole Court believes you and she are enjoying some sort of intimate relations . . . and if I myself, rightly or wrongly, imagine that you and she . . . Say: Yes.

JOHNNY: All right, if it'll make you happier: Yes.

HENRY: No, no, say "yes" without any commentary. Honestly, nobody is listening to us . . . although we are listening to ourselves . . . Say: Yes.

JOHNNY: Yes.

HENRY: Of course, it would be quite simple for me to . . . to do away with you . . . to arrest you as I did with that drunkard. I could even liquidate you, kill you, let's say. But even if I did, it wouldn't change a thing, because . . . because I would always be left with the foreboding suspicion that she really belonged to you and not to me. Say: Yes.

JOHNNY: Yes.

HENRY: These curtains are impossible. I don't understand why this palace is so shabby and poorly kept. There are so many servants around here and still the dirt is everywhere. I have to do something about that. Don't say anything. I'm not finished.
What do you think of me?

JOHNNY: I think you're sick.

HENRY: I'll explain a few things to you, as far as they can be explained.

128

Ever since I became involved in all this, I've been wavering between two poles: between responsibility and irresponsibility, between truth and falsity. On the one hand, I'm convinced that what is going on here is unreal, irresponsible, artificial, cheap. . . . On the other hand, I take all this very seriously and feel as though I bear final responsibility for everything.

I can't refrain from using artificial phrases.

But at the same time these phrases appear less artificial to me than simplicity itself.

I know I am not a real king.
And yet I feel like a king.
I'm enjoying every minute of it.

But at the very same time I know this game is not quite so innocent as it seems. I feel as if, when I pretend something, I actually bring that something into existence, as though with my every word and deed I conjure up and create something . . . something far more powerful than myself.
What do you think of that?

JOHNNY: It's pretty vague.

HENRY: Yes, but you behave at times as though you knew something about it—and so do the others. . . . What do you know? Do you know more or less than I do?

No, I haven't gone crazy. I am a clear-thinking, modern man. Why do I really wish to marry her? Because I'd like to have her as she was before—and I know and I am convinced that if I possessed her without marrying her, I would not be possessing my former fiancée but some worn-out, broken-down slut. . . . I would like this marriage which I'm bestowing upon myself and her to be truly sacred. Does that sound like the idea of a mystic

129

or that of a madman? Or am I incapable of such a sacred act? In the last instance, what is really crucial here? Other people. If others acknowledge the sacredness of that act, then it will be sacred—sacred for them. If they acknowledge her as my chaste and noble Queen, then she will become a queen—for them. And if she's a queen for them, then she's a queen for me.

JOHNNY: Your ideas are sound, but you're making a funny impression on me.

HENRY: Wait a moment. I don't have the power to erase from her past . . . the fact that she was once a whore in some dive . . . and that she once kept company with a lot of drunkards. But if I force everyone, including myself, to accept this solemn marriage which at the same time will have the effect of sanctifying both my love and her honor —then it will be accepted as such. For everything is decided between people! Everything comes from people!

> And now listen
> But listen carefully: as you know, in a moment
> I shall carry out this act . . . I am in need of strength
> But you are weakening me . . .

JOHNNY: Aha.

HENRY: I'll explain my plan of action to you. It's an extremely simple and even dull plan.

I have given orders for everyone to attend a ball at the Royal Court. At this ball, with the help of glances, laughter, caresses, etc. . . . Molly and I will generate between ourselves the greatest amount of love possible. Between ourselves we shall create that love, purity, and fidelity . . . which once existed between us. At the very same time I shall force this pack of fools to pump me full of divinity through tokens of respect and admiration— and then I shall very calmly confer a marriage upon my-

self and her which will legalize and sanctify everything.
. . . What's so strange about that?

Nothing.

Nothing. But you understand that first of all I must
conquer that which is engendered between you . . . and
that which weakens me . . . I am in need of strength.

> But you are depriving me of it . . .
> And now I shall tell you something
> Quite unexpected: you will be obliged
> To kill yourself—and the only reason
> For that is: I command you to do it
> And it is my will . . .

JOHNNY: What a nice proposition!

HENRY: I realize it's a little . . . silly. . . . Do you suppose I'm
not ashamed? This is horribly artificial. But I'm only
saying it . . . by way of a little experiment. . . . I'm merely
curious to see how it sounds—understand? Obviously

> You shouldn't take any of this in earnest
> Who in his right mind, after all, would take it seriously!

It's just that I would like to hear the sound of my own
voice, that's all. But I'd also like to hear how what you are
going to say sounds. Therefore I'll ask you to

> Bow your head and bend your arms and legs, crouch
> down a little
> And say: If that is your will, Henry, then yes, I'd be
> glad to.

JOHNNY: I'm not an actor.

HENRY: Imagine you're learning a poem by heart.

JOHNNY: I don't want to imagine anything.

HENRY: Imagine you're a priest pronouncing the words to some sort of incantation.

JOHNNY: I don't want to imagine anything.

HENRY: Don't you think that a thousand years from now people will be speaking to one another in a completely different fashion from the way we do today?

JOHNNY: That's very possible.

HENRY: And that their conversations will be infinitely richer? There are many melodies which our songbook of today does not contain. What harm can it possibly do you to utter these words by way of a little experiment? And to bow your head?

JOHNNY: What good will it do you if I recite them? Words are not facts.

HENRY: Of course not. No, no, don't think for a moment that I believe in any kind of magical incantations. I am a modern mind. But what harm can it do you to say that . . . and to see how you'll feel while saying it? I'd just like you to get a little taste, a little sample of yourself while you're saying it . . . so you can see what it's like. . . . To a certain extent it can even be thought of in scientific terms. Words evoke certain psychic states in us . . . they create worlds of reality between us. . . . If you said something similar to that . . . something strange . . . then I could say something even stranger and then, by mutually assisting one another, we could go on and on. So you see— it's not quite as difficult or as absurd as it seemed. Two people can do anything. And moreover

> What do you care if something's abnormal
> As long as you are normal!

JOHNNY: All right . . . if it'll make you any happier . . .

132

HENRY: Wait, wait, stand right here beside me. No one can see us, right? No one can see us through the keyhole. This is just between ourselves. Damn it, it's quiet around here! It's as if there was nothing to it, but it's enough to give a person the jitters. Sit down. No, on second thought, stand over here, next to this chair, bow your head

And let your arms droop. Now I'll walk over
To you and stand here beside you and place
My old hand on your young shoulder. It's cold in here!
Chilly, isn't it? I'm touching you . . .

MY DEAREST JOHNNY . . . No, no, that's quite unnecessary . . . there's no need for any prologue . . . YOU MUST KILL YOURSELF BECAUSE THAT IS MY WILL. Now answer the way you were told.

JOHNNY: All right. IF THAT IS YOUR WILL, HENRY, THEN I'D BE GLAD TO.

HENRY: BE PRESENT AT MY WEDDING AND WHEN THE TIME COMES KILL YOURSELF WITH THIS KNIFE. (*He hands him the knife.*)

JOHNNY: VERY WELL.

HENRY: Well, what's new Johnny? Tell me, are they feeding you well at least?

JOHNNY: I can't complain.

HENRY: What time is it?

JOHNNY: Eight-thirty.

HENRY: That watch is worth at least twice the amount you paid for it—if I remember correctly . . .

JOHNNY: I made a good deal on it.

HENRY: It's a good-looking watch. Well, for the time being. Good-bye.

133

JOHNNY: Good-bye. (*He exits.*)

HENRY (*alone*):
> A game
> Let's suppose this is a game
> But . . . what is it really? To what extent can such
>   games be dangerous?
> I would like to know the real capacity of words.
> What is my own capacity?
> A dream? Yes, that's right, a dream . . . child's play . . .

(*To a piece of furniture.*) Are you looking at me? I am
caught in a network of glances, in a precinct of looks,
and everything which I am looking at is looking at me

> Even though I'm alone
> Alone
> Surrounded by this silence . . . I stick out my arm.
>   This ordinary
> Normal
> Commonplace
> Gesture becomes charged with meaning because it's
>   not intended
> For anyone in particular . . .
> I move my fingers in the silence, and my being
> Expands itself to become itself
> The seed of a seed. I, I, I! I alone!
> And yet if I, I, I alone am, why then
> (Let's try that for effect) am I not?

What does it matter (I ask) that I, I am in the very
middle, the very center of everything, if I, I can never be

> Myself?
> I alone.
> I alone.

Now that you're alone, completely alone, you might at
least stop this incessant recitation

Act III

This fabrication of words
This production of gestures

But you, even when you're alone, pretend that you're
alone, and you go on

(For once now let's try to be sincere)

Pretending to be yourself
Even to your very self.

I alone
I alone (Let's emphasize that once more) . . . while out
    there
Nothing but cries, screams and blood, alas, alas, and
    fear
Oh, never before has any man had
To solve such insoluble problems
Or groan under a more awesome burden
Of pain and dishonor . . . How should I view all this?

What attitude should I adopt? Why, why,

In the presence of this vile, inhuman
And disgusting world I might wrinkle my brow
And lift my arms to heaven, I might
Roll my hand into a fist or pass my hand
Across my wise and thoughtful brow
I
Yes, that's right, I . . . Such are the
Attitudes I might adopt . . . in your presence
And for your benefit! But not for my own! I'm not in
    need
Of any attitude! I don't feel
Other people's pain! I only recite
My humanity! No, I do not exist
I haven't any "I," alas, I forge myself
Outside myself, outside myself, alas, alas, oh, the hollow

The Marriage

Empty orchestra of my "alas," you rise up from my
    void
And sink back into the void!

Oh, you demagogues!
(Be vehement, sarcastic when you say that)
Whose mouths are full of morality and
Self-righteousness! (Now grimace
Scornfully, mockingly and make a sweeping gesture
    with your hand)
In vain are all your books and philosophies
Articles and lectures,
Systems and arguments,
Definitions and observations,
Visions, revelations and passions before
Before this mass of two billion people
Who are smothering each other in an eternal,
Dark and shapeless, untamed lust . . .
In vain does your fly buzz about the nose
Of that green and black abyss (Now let your laughter
    resound
Your private and discreet
Quiet and ineffable
Humanly human laughter . . .) While you out there
Persist in your endless posing
We go on pinching ourselves here in our own little way
Underneath the bushes of our destiny.

(And now, to bring
This monologue to a close)

I reject every order, every concept
I distrust every abstraction, every doctrine
I don't believe in God or in Reason!
Enough of these gods! Give me man!
May he be like me, troubled and immature
Confused and incomplete, dark and obscure

So I can dance with him! Play with him! Fight with
   him!
Pretend to him! Ingratiate myself with him!
And rape him, love him and forge myself
Anew from him, so I can grow through him, and in
   that way
Celebrate my marriage in the sacred human church!

From all sides enter the DIGNITARIES, LADIES, CHANCELLOR,
CHIEF OF POLICE. *Music, ball.*

CHORUS:
> *The quadrille has begun, let every voice ring!*
> *Long live His Majesty, His Majesty the King!*

HENRY:
> *The quadrille has begun, let every voice ring!*

CHANCELLOR:
> *Long live His Majesty, His Majesty the King!*

HENRY (*strolling arm in arm with the* CHANCELLOR):
> Look, my good fellow, look how they dance!
> Lulled by the chorus into a wondrous trance
> Oh, the sweet perfume that dreams engender
> Oh, 'tis a night of golden-haired splendor . . .

CHANCELLOR:
> This quadrille is stately in the extreme
> It helps to sweeten our every dream
> The soul takes wing, it leaves no tracks
> Its hair is as golden as newly spun flax!

HENRY:
> Though the sense be lacking, let rhyme abound
> The sweet smoke of hopes vain and unsound
> Let rhythm and rhyme spin merrily 'round
> In an unending circle as far as Capetown!

Pooh! Pooh! Pooh!

That's enough! Stop!

The GUESTS *stop dancing.*

Tell them to bow!

They do so.

Once more!

They bow again.

Once more!

They bow again.

These bows are inflating me. . . . Where are my men? (*The* HENCHMEN *come in.*) I swear they are a frightful lot, amen. Where is the Chief of Police? (CHIEF *comes forward.*) You and your men are to grab everything and everybody by the snout, amen. If anyone so much as dares to . . . lay a finger on me . . . pounce on him at once. Now then. (*Walking among the* GUESTS *and scrutinizing them.*) Is everybody here? That old battle-axe—who is she?

CHANCELLOR: That's Princess Pirulu.

HENRY: I knew she was a princess the moment I laid eyes on her—she's so vulgar-looking. And that moron?

CHANCELLOR: He's a supreme moron.

HENRY: There's a moronic look in his eye. And who's that flabby, sweaty-looking character with the potbelly and the white skin?

CHANCELLOR: A gourmet.

HENRY: He has a pimple behind his ear. What exactly does he taste?

CHANCELLOR: His own distaste.

HENRY: Good. I see you've brought me the cream of the crop. (*To a* HENCHMAN, *pointing to the* GOURMET.) Step on his foot—but good and hard so it hurts.

Quiet.

It's quiet here, isn't it? (*Glancing around the room.*) The very elite, indeed. It's quite evident they represent the highest circles of this illustrious kingdom. But why are they all so old? This is a congress of geezers!

CHANCELLOR: I beg your pardon, Sire.

HENRY: But these are not people! These are caricatures! Just look at all these spectacles, goatees and mustaches—how it disgusts me to look at all these shrivelled-up, emaciated bodies—these pitiful, sclerotic and despondent varicose veins, fallen arches, sagging breasts, protruding bellies, false teeth, this inertia, sclerosis, atrophy, these infirmities and maladies, defects and blemishes, and all this hideous, shameful nakedness! And moreover how distinguished they look, coddled, pampered and fawned upon by the most chic hairdressers! Hey, corpse, show me your sock: my but that's an exquisite sock, such a tasteful color and made of the finest silk too—what an elegant piece of hose! Only your foot is in a state of decomposition. These are people already in the process of disintegrating. They have a cemetery look about them. And these are the people who govern?

GUESTS (*dancing*):
The quadrille has begun, let every voice ring!
Long live His Majesty, His Majesty the King!

They stop dancing. Enter the LACKEYS *with trays loaded down with bottles.*

LACKEYS: Burgundy, Tokay, Malaga, port!

HENRY (*without taking his eyes off the* GUESTS): What a revelry of faces! What a debauchery of noses and bellies! What an orgy of baldness!

> Orchestra of unbridled ugliness
> Some music for my wedding! This licentiousness suits my purpose.

LACKEYS: Burgundy, Tokay, Malaga, port!

HENRY: Where is my fiancée?

CHANCELLOR: Here she comes now with those maidens dressed all in white.

HENRY: Let her approach and let her smile at me and lower her eyes as she bows before me. I shall bow and taking her gently by the shoulders I shall prevent her from kneeling down, at the same time I shall smile at her the way I used to do in former times. (*He and* MOLLY *do so.*)

CHANCELLOR (*aside*): Your Majesty, everyone is listening.

HENRY (*loudly*): That's precisely what I want them to do. We don't love one another—we merely engender the feeling of love between us. . . . (*To* MOLLY.) Why aren't you smiling? Smile at me, the way you did before you were raped and became a slut for some barkeeper, understand? Otherwise, I'll let you have it. And don't look around— don't try to catch anyone else's glance—you know I'm jealous of Johnny. (*To the* CHANCELLOR.) I'm deliberately saying all this out loud because there's no need to conceal anything here; here everything is in the open. Look how graciously she's smiling. That smile evokes within me a multitude of memories and moves me in the presence . . . in the presence of all these people . . .

> My darling, if only your smile
> Would reverberate off them and come back to me

In waves a hundred times stronger . . .
Trust in me, have no fear, I shall find a way
To fill the void of my heart
And I shall love you again, as
I loved you once before.

Let her squeeze my hand in secret. All right. Now what?
What should we do now, Chamberlain, to make this a
truly royal reception?

CHAMBERLAIN (*announces*):
Circle.
Circle.
Circle.

LACKEYS: Port!

The GUESTS *group themselves into small circles.*

CHAMBERLAIN: With your leave, Sire, with your leave, Sire,
with your leave, Sire, the most illustrious names, the
greatest fortunes, the highest offices, the very flower, the
very elite, the very cream, in short, Your Majesty, everyone—dreams of nothing else save the honor to kiss your
hand, Sire. I have the honor! I have the honor! I have
the honor to present to His Majesty our renowned poet
Paul Valéry, the undisputed pride and glory of mankind
. . . and the poet Rainer Maria Rilke, likewise the pride
and glory of mankind. Men of genius! Immortal! In-
comparable!

HENRY: Let them pay homage to me. (*To* MOLLY.) Take my
arm.
Why are those old ladies bowing to one another and
not to me? I'm going to blow myself up and squish out
their guts!

Who gave any of you permission to clown around?
There'll be no fooling around in my presence!

141

CHAMBERLAIN: One moment, Your Majesty, forgive me, Your Majesty. . . . Before rendering homage to you, they must first of all affirm their own greatness by bowing before each other.

HENRY: This one must be having trouble with his kidneys! What do you mean they must bow before each other?

CHAMBERLAIN: It's just that the greatness and profundity of these two unrivaled poets cannot be fully appreciated by anybody except themselves. Since all the others are lesser poets, they are equally incompetent to judge or appreciate or understand them. Therefore, by exchanging bows with each other they are testifying to one another's greatness, which they will then place at His Majesty's feet.

The POETS *bow before* HENRY.

CHANCELLOR: Oh, heaven help us . . .

HENRY: Good. The glory of these two melancholy lute players is now a part of me. Keep on pumping. Who's that long-haired imbecile over there?

CHAMBERLAIN: A pianist.

HENRY: Why are all those senile old biddies squirming around over there goggle-eyed, madly clutching their shrivelled-up breasts?

CHAMBERLAIN: Women always go into convulsions in the company of an actor, singer, or virtuoso.

HENRY: These are just the sort of second-rate gods I need. Tell this guy to pump his divinity into me with a bow. He hasn't got much longer to live anyway—he's a consumptive. Just look at those delicate fingers. And this old hag? Why is the scullion arranging a kneeling rail in front of her?

Act III

CHANCELLOR: Oh, heaven help us . . .

CHAMBERLAIN: With your leave, Sire . . . forgive me, Sire, it's just that the Princess, as Your Majesty has already been pleased to remark, is a rather vulgar woman. She would give anything to fall down on her knees before Your Majesty, but her knees are . . .

HENRY (*lifting up her skirt*): Hm . . . as a matter of fact . . . she is a little on the dumpy side . . .

CHAMBERLAIN: Yes, but she has a servant girl and this servant girl will render her knees honorable before they render homage to Your Majesty.

HENRY: To tell you the truth, I would prefer the knees of this young wench.

A LACKEY (*pouring the wine*): Burgundy!

CHAMBERLAIN: No, that's impossible! She's this woman's servant.

CHANCELLOR: Her servant. At her service!

HENRY (*to a* LADY): What's your name?

LADY: Gertrude.

HENRY: What are you dying from, excuse me, I mean, what are you living on?

LADY: A pension.

HENRY: What do you occupy yourself with?

LADY: My feeble condition.

HENRY: What are you living for?

LADY: To enjoy everybody's respect.

HENRY: This woman is a goddess. An altar adorned with precious jewels and perfumed by the servant girl. Let her kneel down before me on this kneeling rail and let her servant kiss her on the heel. Now start pumping! Oh, how I'm itching! Damn this itching—Chamberlain, scratch me just above my left shoulder blade.

CHAMBERLAIN: Here?

HENRY: No, higher, to the left.

CHAMBERLAIN: Here?

HENRY: No, to the right. Oh, what's the difference. But it annoys me . . .

CHAMBERLAIN (*in a confidential manner*): It annoys you?

CHANCELLOR (*curious*): Does it annoy you?

HENRY: It's nothing, nothing at all. It's even amusing. Where is my father? Show my ex-father in here along with my late mother. We're going to begin right away. (*To* MOLLY.) Squeeze my fingers and I'll squeeze yours. . . . But the place is so empty. It seems as if there's nobody here.

I am alone.
Together with you . . .

MOLLY: I love you . . .

HENRY: That's right, say that, say that out loud so everybody, everybody, everybody can hear. (*To the* CHANCELLOR.) Where is my father? Show that drunkard in too!

CHANCELLOR (*in a perfunctory manner*): Your father will be here soon.

HENRY: (*in a perfunctory manner*): Why isn't my father here?

CHANCELLOR (*as above*): He'll be here soon.

HENRY (*as above*): If he's going to be here, let him be here.

144

Act III

CHANCELLOR (*as above*): Soon it will be that your father will be here.

The FATHER *and* MOTHER *along with the* DRUNKARD *are carried in by the* HENCHMEN *and thrown at Henry's feet.*

HENRY: Now what?

CHANCELLOR: Nothing.

CHIEF: Nothing.

HENRY: Nothing.

The same bunch I knelt before a little while ago.

He nudges his parents with his foot.

I don't know . . .
I could eat something . . .

FATHER: I could eat something too.

MOTHER: So could I.

HENRY: For the time being though there isn't anything to eat.

MOTHER: Well, if there isn't anything, there isn't anything.

FATHER: Do you remember, Henry, how we used to go for drives in the country together in the wagon?

MOLLY: And I sometimes went along too when the weather was nice.

HENRY: It's true—we had some pleasant outings together. . . . (*He stands up.*) But that's beside the point. Completely beside the point! This is not the time for chit-chat . . . I have to grant myself a marriage!

CHANCELLOR: Grant yourself a marriage!

HENRY: Burgundy!

A LACKEY: Burgundy!

HENRY:
>Burgundy!
>Hey, Chamberlain, let's empty this goblet
>In honor of my lady!

CHAMBERLAIN: Burgundy!

CHANCELLOR: Burgundy!

A LACKEY: Burgundy!

HENRY:
>To the health
>Of my loyal subjects!

GUESTS (*raising their goblets*):
>Long live His Majesty the King!

LACKEYS (*raising their wine trays*):
>Burgundy! Burgundy! Burgundy!

GUESTS (*dancing*):
>*The quadrille has begun, let every voice ring!*
>*Long live His Majesty, His Majesty the King!*
>*Under the spell of this enchanting wine*
>*May the spell of this ball reach limits sublime!*

HENRY (*strolling with* MOLLY):
>O 'tis a night of magical splendors
>Illusory is the power that love engenders
>The dreamlike waft of eternal illusions
>And the melancholy music of nostalgic allusions!

MOLLY:
>Oh, the tears I once shed for my maidenly dreams
>A petal adrift on a sea of timid sighs
>The lilacs of the past are in bloom again it seems
>And the brother I feared lost is standing before my
>>eyes.

Act III

HENRY:
> Look how gracefully they dance the quadrille!
> It's a dance that's designed to give a man a thrill
> And instruct the human heart in love and good will . . .
> Enough! Enough! Stop!
> (*To a* LACKEY.) Burgundy!

A LACKEY: Burgundy!

HENRY: Burgundy!

A LACKEY: Burgundy!

HENRY (*advancing toward the crowd*):
> Get out of my way!
> Move back! I'm advancing
> Toward you! This is my person!
> It is I, I alone! Space!
> Let there be space! It is I who am here!
> Here, in the very center of everything!
> And now watch carefully!

Move one of those empty chairs over here. And have her sit down on it.

Now I'll walk up to her and . . . and then what? And then I'll touch her, for example. I'll touch her . . . I'll touch her with this finger . . . and that will mean we are married and that henceforth she is my legitimate, legal, faithful, chaste, and innocent spouse. I don't need any other ceremonies. I can invent my own ceremonies. And as soon as I touch her, you are to fall down on your knees and by the very fact of kneeling down you will elevate my touch to the level of a holiness most holy . . . to the level of a nuptial ceremony . . .

Do you dare not to go down on your knees? Do you dare not to consecrate this marriage by kneeling down? Now on with it, on with it, come on, let's go, let's go, oh Henry, Henry, Henry!

The Marriage

COURT:

Henry, Henry, Henry!
On with it! On with it! Oh, Henry, Henry, Henry!

HENRY:

I don't give a damn
What any of you may be thinking! But . . . what are
you thinking?
Do you think that . . . that what? (*To a* LADY.) What are
you thinking?

LADY: I'm not thinking anything.

HENRY: Yes, you are, you're thinking and that goes for the
rest of you too.

A LACKEY: Port!

CHANCELLOR: They're thinking.

CHIEF: They're thinking . . . everyone is thinking . . .

HENRY (*thoughtfully*): They're thinking . . . (*He goes from
guest to guest, looking each in the face; he bumps into*
JOHNNY.) Oh, Johnny, how are you?

JOHNNY: All right.

HENRY: What's new?

JOHNNY: Not much.

HENRY: Good. (*They remain standing opposite one another.*)

CHANCELLOR:

His Majesty
Seems curiously absorbed . . .

CHIEF:

Yes, the King is absorbed . . .

HENRY (*to himself*):

I don't want to drink any more . . .

148

I'm not going to drink any more . . .
(*To everyone.*)
Are you perhaps thinking
That I am able to rule here solely because
They are shackled . . . That I could not
Stand up to them if they were released? . . .
(*To the* CHANCELLOR.)
So be it then!
Untie these prisoners and let them attack
Me!

CHANCELLOR: Sire!

CHIEF: Sire!

HENRY (*to* JOHNNY):
You know
What's expected of you!
(*Aloud.*)
Come on! Untie them! Let's make it clear
Once and for all who is in command here!

The MOTHER *and* FATHER *stand up. Now for the first time it is possible to see the frightful state this couple is in as their bloody, swollen faces gradually become visible.*

HENRY:
What buffoonery!
Oh, how frightfully artificial! All the same, this artificiality
Is frightful!

CHANCELLOR: They look as though they just got out of prison.

HENRY:
Are you trying to frighten me?
Why don't you go ahead and attack me?
Nothing?

149

CHANCELLOR: Nothing.

CHIEF: Nothing.

DIGNITARY/TRAITOR: Nothing.

A group of TRAITORS *approaches with evil intentions.*

HENRY: Henchmen, get over here!

The HENCHMEN *come over and stand directly behind him.*

> If they attack
> Me, you attack them . . . But
> Why don't they attack?

CHANCELLOR: Nothing.

CHIEF: Nothing.

DIGNITARY/TRAITOR: Nothing.

CHAMBERLAIN: Nothing.

HENRY:

> I am not ashamed
> I don't feel any pity for you
> Nor am I afraid of you
> No, no . . . I merely have to back down from them
> As though I were afraid, as though I were ashamed . . .
> I wonder what they're up to?

CHANCELLOR: Nothing.

CHIEF: Nothing.

CHAMBERLAIN: Nothing.

HENRY:

> Ohh, here they come!
> What do you want? What do you want?

He runs up to the FATHER, *but does not dare touch him.*

150

You pig!

DRUNKARD (*violently, off to one side*): You pig!

HENRY (*to the* DRUNKARD): You pig!

> HENRY *and the* DRUNKARD *come down to the front of the stage.*

DRUNKARD:
> Pig!
> You piggish pigmonger pig of a slut
> Hoggish boar of a greasy porker!

HENRY:
> Sow of a souse!

DRUNKARD:
> Prick of a pig!

HENRY:
> Swine!

FATHER:
> Oh, what a pigsty, what a pigsty!

LACKEYS:
> Oh, Burgundy, Burgundy, Burgundy!

DRUNKARD:
> Piggish pig!
> Your girl friend is a slut of a sow! Oink! Oink! Oink!

HENRY:
> You're a pig yourself!
> You pig, pig, pig!

GUESTS:
> Oh, what a pig!

LACKEYS:
> Oh, Burgundy, Burgundy, Burgundy!

HENRY:

>Idiot
>You're an idiot!

DRUNKARD:

>You're the one who's an idiot,
>You idiot! You dried-up tit of a sow!

HENRY:

>Pig puss!

DRUNKARD:

>You're a pig!
>A piggified pig!
>A piggish, piggicized, piggerized superpig!
>Piggy-wiggy! Oink! Oink! Oink!

HENRY:

>Pig!

MOTHER: He's grunting like a hog!

CHIEF: He's drooling like a dog!

FATHER: Oh, what swine, oh, what swine!

LACKEYS: Oh, what wine, oh, what wine!

HENRY:

>You boar
>Just try and touch me!

DRUNKARD:

>And I will toushh you
>I'll toushh you yet, I'll toushh you yet
>And then I'll blow myself up and blow this pig down,
>Squish out his guts and spit all over him! *Ain't that
>   right, Miss Molly?*

Quiet.

>Do you see this Finnger?

HENRY:

    Say whatever you please
    I'm not afraid . . .

DRUNKARD:

    Fellow citizens!

    I ain't an educated man, but I got eyes . . . and I see
they're fixin' to have themselves a pretty hifalutin' wedding. . . . But what I keep wonderin' is—how can they go
through with it, with the wedding I mean, when the
bride has already been . . . ahem . . . married to someone
else? . . .

    Do you see this Finnger?
    Look at my Finnger!
    Don't look at anything else but my Finnger!

HENRY: But it's tickling me!

DRUNKARD: Don't look at anything else but my Finnger!

HENRY:

    I've got goose pimples
    All over me . . .

DRUNKARD: Look carefully at my Finnger. Look in which direction of the room it's pointing . . .

HENRY: I feel like laughing . . .

DRUNKARD: Look at how my Finnger's pointing at something
over there behind those Personages. . . . There's a young
man over there. . . . Look how I'm pointing with my
Finnger in his direction. . . . In a second the shame of
this royal family will be made public . . .

HENRY:

    This display
    Is shamelessly
    Touching my Person . . .

DRUNKARD (*shouting*):
>The King is a cuckold
>His fiancée has been carrying on behind his back!
>Step aside
>And you will see the fellow
>Who's been playing footsie with her!
>There he is, in back of the guests!

The GUESTS *make way, revealing* JOHNNY'S CORPSE.

CHANCELLOR: Dead.

CHIEF: Murdered.

FATHER: A corpse.

MOTHER: Dead.

CHAMBERLAIN: A corpse.

DRUNKARD (*startled*):
>A corpse!
>I'll be d . . . Stabbed with a knife . . .
>Who stabbed him?

A GUEST (*to* HENRY):
>Sire!
>He stabbed himself!

DRUNKARD:
>He killed himself? But why?

HENRY:
>On my orders . . .

ALL:
>The King, the King!

HENRY:
>But . . . is this for real?
>(*A moment later.*)
>Put something under his head.

Act III

ALL:

The King, the King!

HENRY: Who would ever have believed it? It's only a dream. It's even extremely artificial. And yet he's lying here

And she is standing over there
And here am I.
(*A moment later.*)
Now I can grant myself a marriage!

ALL:

The King, the King, oh, Henry, Henry, Henry!

LACKEYS:

O Burgundy, Burgundy, Burgundy!

HENRY: Who would have ever believed it? It's nothing but a dream. The whole thing is even extremely artificial. And yet he's lying there

And she is standing over there

(*Lowering his voice.*) I'll walk over to her now and make out of her what I damn well please. . . . I'm going to take her and marry her . . . with all my power . . .

But what was it I wanted to say?

There was something I wanted to say, but now I've forgotten what it was.

Let's see, what was it? . . . Oh, yes! It seems there isn't going to be any marriage because . . .

I don't feel like it any more
(*To* MOLLY.) I'm sorry . . .

CHANCELLOR (*upstage, bent over* JOHNNY): He's got bloodstains all over his shirt . . .

FATHER: Well, no one can bring him back to life now.

MOTHER: He must have been insane! At first I thought it was

155

just a joke . . . but when I saw the way he was lying on the ground . . .

DRUNKARD: There's no point in talking about it any more. . . . He's done for. Finished.

HENRY:

Oh, I know perfectly well it isn't true!
And yet . . .
Ladies
And gentlemen
Kneel down and bow your heads
Because instead of a wedding . . . there's going to be a
    funeral!

CHANCELLOR: A funeral.

FATHER: Well, if there's got to be a funeral, there's got to be one, I guess.

HENRY:

Lay him down over here. (*To* MOLLY.) You stand over
    here beside him.
This corpse is my creation
But this creation is incomprehensible
Dark
Obscure . . .
More powerful than I, and
Perhaps not even my own!
Form a funeral procession!

CHANCELLOR: It's a funeral march!

FATHER: It's a funeral march!

HENRY:

No! I'm not responsible for anything here!
I don't understand my own words!
I have no control over my own deeds!
I know nothing, nothing, nothing, I understand
    nothing, nothing, nothing!

Whoever says he understands is a liar!
You don't know anything
Any more than I do!

Being mutually united, we are forever arranging ourselves into new forms
And these forms well up from below. What a peculiar
haze! An inexplicable melody! A delirious dance! An
ambiguous march!

And an earthly human church
Whose priest I am!

DRUNKARD: Whose priest I am . . .

FATHER (*tenderly*): Henry . . .

MOTHER (*tenderly*): Henry . . .

HENRY:

I am innocent.

I declare that I am as innocent as a child, that I have done
nothing, that I am ignorant of everything . . .

No one is responsible for anything here!
There is no such thing as responsibility!

If, however, there is a corpse, then there has to be a
funeral, and if there has to be a funeral, then four of you
must stand next to him so you can raise him up at a
signal from me . . .

No, there is no responsibility
Still, there are formalities
To be attended to . . .

Four of the DIGNITARIES *come over and stand next to*
JOHNNY'S CORPSE.

If, however, four of you are standing over there, next
to him, then four of you must stand over here, next to me.

157

He and I . . . Four and four . . . On this side and on that side . . .

MOTHER: My child, don't get yourself all upset, never mind about all this, Henry darling, I'm your mother after all. Can't you talk normally any more? Can't you give me a simple kiss?

HENRY:

No. Nobody can speak to anybody in a normal manner.
In vain do you struggle to get free of yourself in order
    to reach me, and
In vain do I struggle to get free of myself to reach all
    of you

Yes, I'm imprisoned . . .

I am a prisoner
Even though I am innocent . . . What was it I wanted
    to say?
While I am standing here
And speaking . . .
Let your hands . . .
Touch . . . me . . .

The GUARDS *who are standing behind him place their hands on his shoulders.*

Wait a minute.
I'm not through yet.

If I am imprisoned here, then somewhere, somewhere far away, let this deed of mine be raised up on high.

They lift up JOHNNY'S CORPSE.

And now let this funeral march of yours
Carry you away!

Procession.